RACING
THE
PAST

RACING THE PAST

Sis Deans

Henry Holt and Company ▪ New York

Acknowledgments

I would like to thank college runners Bridget and Brian MacLaughlin for reading the novel and sharing their insightful comments and running expertise. Special thanks go to writers John Cofran and Wanda Poore Whitten for their friendship and years of support. I would also like to thank my agent, Upton Brady, for believing in me; my editor at Henry Holt, Reka Simonsen, for all her hard work; and my copyeditor, Terry Evans-Zaroff, for her attention to detail. And to my nieces and nephews, Deana, Amanda, Maryella, Caleb, and Matthew, who are all track and cross-country runners, thank you for the inspiration—keep on running!

Henry Holt and Company, LLC, *Publishers since 1866*
115 West 18th Street, New York, New York 10011

Henry Holt is a registered trademark of Henry Holt and Company, LLC
Copyright © 2001 by Sis Deans. All rights reserved.
Published in Canada by Fitzhenry & Whiteside Ltd.,
195 Allstate Parkway, Markham, Ontario L3R 4T8.

Library of Congress Cataloging-in-Publication Data
Deans, Sis Boulos. Racing the past / Sis Deans   p.   cm.
Summary: After the death of his abusive father, eleven-year-old Ricky tries
to help his younger brother deal with his residual fears and discovers that
running helps him deal with his own anger and the taunts of a bullying classmate.
[1. Child abuse—Fiction.   2. Fathers and sons—Fiction.   3. Brothers—Fiction.
4. Running—Fiction.]   I. Title. PZ7.D3514 Rac 2001   [Fic]—dc21   00-61349

ISBN 0-8050-6635-7 / First Edition—2001 / Designed by Donna Mark
Printed in the United States of America on acid-free paper. ∞

1   2   3   4   5   6   7   8   9   10

For
John, Jessie, Rachel, and Emma

RACING
THE
PAST

... *Chapter One*

From where he sat in the principal's office, eleven-year-old Ricky Gordon could see the empty swings in the playground rocking in the breeze. Fifteen minutes ago, beneath that blue sky that felt more like May than the first day of March, he'd gotten in a fight with Bugsie McCarthy, a sixth-grader twice his size. *My father said the best thing your father ever did for your family was running his truck off of Dead Man's Curve.* Although Ricky secretly agreed, Bugsie had no right to say it, so he'd attacked the bigger boy with wild, flying punches. It was a fight he'd lost, and as if to confirm it, he ran his tongue over his swollen, salty lip.

Mr. Daniels, the principal of Harmony Elementary, tapped his silver pen on the desk mat in front of him. "I'm getting tired of seeing you in that chair, Richard."

Not as tired as I am, thought Ricky.

"This is the sixth time you've been in my office this

year for fighting." The principal gave the desk mat a harder rap. "The sixth!"

"The seventh," Ricky corrected automatically.

"I hope that wasn't meant to be a joke."

"No, sir, it's just . . . it's the seventh, not the sixth."

"It's nothing to be proud of either way."

Ricky didn't respond; he usually didn't. He wouldn't have spoken up a moment ago, but he couldn't let Daniels' mistake pass; he had too great a respect for numbers. There was something clean and real about numbers. They were exact; they didn't lie.

"Now, I think I've been very lenient with you up to this point, Richard. I know you've had a hard time lately with your father's death and everything, but I can't let this behavior continue on my premises. Someone's going to be hurt, and I am ultimately responsible for that. . . ."

Ricky watched the second hand revolve around the clock. Cripe, he'd already lost twelve minutes of math. Even though he was only in fifth grade, Mr. Garvey had him working at the seventh-grade level.

". . . One bad apple will spoil the whole barrel, Richard. . . ."

If it takes 1 bad apple 2 days to spoil 4 apples, how long will it take to spoil a barrel of 84? Ricky wondered. By day 2, there'd be 5 spoiled apples; in a couple of days they each spoil 4, then those 25 . . .

". . . And, frankly, I don't want any bad apples in my barrel . . ."

4

Less than a week to spoil every kid in the whole school!

"... There are certain rules the students of this school must follow. ..."

If the bad apple got paid 50¢ a head for spoiling all those apples, how much would he be paid?

"Rule number one! There is no, I repeat, no fighting on the premises. ..."

$42 or ...

"Are you listening to me, Richard?"

... 33 comic books and 75¢ left over—not including tax.

"This is exactly what I'm talking about, Richard. You haven't heard a word I've said. Because of your family situation I've been reluctant to call your mother in, but now I see I have to get her involved. If you won't listen to me, maybe you'll listen to her."

A jolt of protectiveness straightened Ricky's shoulders. "You can't do that, Mr. Daniels," he pleaded. "My mother's got enough to worry about."

"I'm afraid I don't have a choice."

Ricky's mind raced wildly. Already he could see the hurt in his mother's eyes, hear the disappointment in her voice as she said, *You promised me.* "Listen, Mr. Daniels, I'll make you a deal."

The pen hesitated in midair; then the principal asked in disbelief, "A deal?"

"You said you didn't want any fighting on your premises, right?"

"Exactly."

"Well, if you don't call my mother in, I'll give up recess, and when I get to school in the morning, I'll go right to my classroom. That way, the only time I could get in a fight on your premises would be in class, and that wouldn't happen, 'cause Bugsie ain't in my class."

Mr. Daniels leaned back in his chair, shaking his head, a small smile lifting the corners of his mustache. "You'd do that?"

"If you don't call my mother in, I'll do it."

Mr. Daniels resumed drumming the pen as he thought. "If this doesn't work out, Richard, or if you end up in that chair again for any reason, I'll have to call her. Is that clear?"

"Yes, sir."

"You may leave now. And please tell Mr. McCarthy to come in on your way out."

Ricky closed the door behind him, then glanced at Bugsie, who was sitting on the black bench outside of Mr. Daniels' office. "He's ready for you," said Ricky, trying to avoid the older boy's glare.

"And I'll be ready for *you* on the bus, Gordon," said Bugsie, punching his right hand into the palm of his left.

Ricky looked up sharply, the anger he'd felt on the playground washing over him anew. His urge to hurt Bugsie was so powerful that he could envision his hands squeezing that thick neck, could see Bugsie's freckled face turning blue and his bugged-out eyes rolling like marbles in their sockets.

6

"Out of my way, wimp," said Bugsie, shoving by him.

It was enough to snap Ricky out of his fantasy, but for just a fraction of a second, as he watched the bully's strutting figure disappear into the principal's office, it amazed him that Bugsie was still alive and able to walk. Slowly, Ricky looked down at his clenched hands, and it was only then that he realized how difficult it was going to be to keep his deal with Mr. Daniels.

· · ■ · ·

Lyle Benson, Ricky's one and only friend, looked uncertainly at the school bus that was preparing to leave. "You can't walk home, Ricky. . . ."

Ricky stood beside Lyle, searching the windows of the yellow bus for his little brother's face. He'd already informed Matt he was walking—had told him at lunch, "If I get on that bus there'll be trouble, and I can't afford it."

". . . it's more than five miles," Lyle continued, pleading his case.

"Three and a half," said Ricky. "And I'm walking. You do what you want."

"But if you don't take the bus, all the kids will think you're chicken of Bugsie."

"I don't give a rat's turd what they think," Ricky countered. He spotted Matt, who had his face squished against the window so that his lips looked like a brook trout's, his nose like a pig's. Ricky started laughing and gave him the thumbs-up sign for the funny face and for sitting up front, just like Ricky had told him to.

Lyle jabbed at his thick glasses until they rested squarely on his pug nose. "If I ain't home for milking, my old man will kick my butt all over the barn," he said nervously.

"Catch the bus then," Ricky snapped; he slung his backpack over his shoulder and stepped off the curb. When he reached the other side of the driveway, he turned around in time to see Lyle running for the bus. Ricky's stomach sank as he watched the bus lurch forward with a burp of exhaust. He thought Lyle had deserted him, but after the bus passed by, there was his friend, standing on the sidewalk, coughing and fanning away a black cloud of fumes.

A smile tore at Ricky's sore lip. "You going to stand there all day or what?"

Lyle started walking toward him with a martyred look on his face. "You owe me," he said.

Ricky didn't like owing anybody anything—not even his best friend. "This will make up for all the times I do your math homework," he told him.

Lyle jabbed at his glasses, then shot a wary look toward the bus that was already at the stop sign. "For someone who's so smart in math, you sure are stupid," he said. "Bugsie's gonna lap this up like a dog. Heck, he'll probably use it against you the rest of the year."

"A hundred-percent chance of that," Ricky agreed, then started walking across the empty playground, where patches of snow still clung to the mud and rust-colored grass.

"Never heard of anyone crazy enough to tangle with Bugsie," said Lyle, awe tingeing his nasal voice. "His whole gang's gonna be gunning for you. You won't be able to use the boys' room till September."

Ricky glanced down at his friend tagging along beside him. Lyle was the runt of the Benson family—short, spindly, always sick with asthma. "Any more good news?" he asked him.

Lyle was silent for a moment. "Yeah," he finally said. "Next year, Bugsie and his boys will be going to the junior high. We won't have to see that skid's face on the bus till we're in seventh grade."

Ricky and Lyle cut into the woods, following the narrow muddy path edged with white oak. Many of the grayish-white trunks had been carved with initials, hearts, and dates by students past and present at Harmony Elementary. On one tree, just below where the trunk turned into a V, Ricky's parents' initials were connected with a plus sign. More than once he'd been tempted to find a sharp rock and erase those scars from the tree, but something had always kept him from it—perhaps the fear that his father might find out.

Today, however, he passed by the tree without giving it a glance or a thought. His eyes were trained on the dirt trail in front of him, which was bedded with wet brown leaves and remnants of last year's acorns, his mind on what he was going to tell his mother. He had to have a good excuse to explain away his fat lip;

there was no way he could tell her what Bugsie had said on the playground loud enough for Matt and everyone to hear.

The way his mother had been acting lately, Ricky wasn't sure what she'd do. Before his father had gotten killed, she'd never dared to say anything and hardly ever went out of the house. Back then, he could always trust her with his secrets. *We have to make sure your father doesn't find out, or you'll feel the back of his belt for sure.*

But now that his father was dead, his mother was breaking all the rules. She'd gotten a job sewing up at Mrs. Chaffee's and had started going grocery shopping with his aunts, who, when his father was alive, were never supposed to come over to the house. With her new haircut, she didn't even look the same. It was like he had a different mother, and now that they had a phone again, he was afraid that his new mother might even call up Mr. McCarthy if she knew the truth about what had happened on the playground. That's all I'd need, thought Ricky, Bugsie after me for that on top of everything else.

The thing was, Bugsie was right. Getting killed *was* the best thing his father had ever done for them. On New Year's Day, when "Our Cop," the town constable, woke them up to break the news, Ricky had felt so relieved he'd had to stop himself from singing out loud—*Ding-dong, the old man's dead!*

And at the wake, while all those grown-ups were walking back and forth in front of the casket pretending they were sorry, he'd just sat in a metal chair thinking about how nice it was going to be to go home and not find his father passed out on the couch. There would be no more running to the neighbors in the middle of the night in his underwear to call for help. No more lying in bed listening to the clink of beer bottles. No wondering what was going to set him off this time—potato chips eaten too loudly, a supper that wasn't hot enough, a misplaced screwdriver. No more of him. Ever.

As the two boys left the school woods behind and prepared to cross Route 26, Lyle sang "Hi ho, hi ho, off the *premises* we go."

It was enough to derail Ricky's train of thought, and he started laughing.

The smile on Lyle's face broadened. "Bet Daniels said that word a few million times when he had you in his office."

"No kidding," said Ricky. "That's his favorite word. But you have to Scouts' Honor you won't tell anyone about the deal I made with him."

Although Lyle had quit Scouts right after Ricky had been kicked out, they both continued to use Scouts' Honor on serious matters. Without hesitation, Lyle raised his two fingers. "Scouts' Honor," he said, then asked, "What about your lip? Your mother's gonna want to know how you got that."

Ricky touched his lip with a gentle finger. "I'll make up something," he said. "Maybe I got hit with a baseball at recess."

11

"Believable," said Lyle. "And it wouldn't be a whole lie, 'cause Bugsie did *hit* you at recess."

"At least I won't have to lie to her about the bus," said Ricky, easing his conscience more. "Even walking, I'll be home before she is. The only way she'd find out is if Matt told her, and he'd never do that." He and Matt always covered for each other. Their father used to say, "One lies and the other one swears to it." It was probably the only truthful thing their father ever said.

Ricky and Lyle walked along Route 26 for a quarter of a mile, sticking to the soft shoulder, then turned onto Ridge Road, which would eventually lead them home. The afternoon sun was warm on their shoulders, and a mingled scent of earth and manure wafted up at them. As they ambled down the country road that snaked its way past woods, fields, Hatchet Mountain, and a scattering of houses, the weight of Ricky's troubles seemed to grow a little lighter.

At the Bakers' farm pond the winter ice had already disappeared, and they stopped to throw rocks into the murky water. At the Williamses', whom Ricky's father used to call "them stupid city slickers," they spent a few minutes visiting with a golden retriever who'd run up the driveway. And by Slowpoke Clara's, who always seemed to take an hour getting on or off the bus, they found a dime. Ricky was just starting to think that walking home wasn't so bad when he heard the first faint rumble of the bus.

Both boys veered toward the side of the road, then turned and looked behind them as the bus, which had already made its loop around Mountain Road, rounded the bend and came into view. The bus picked up speed as the road straightened, the whining of its shifting gears making Ricky reach out to pull Lyle a little closer to the ditch. He braced himself as the yellow vehicle grew larger. It barreled by, its big wheels spitting sand into the hot tailwind, and he heard someone yell, "Hope you make it home before darrrk!"

Ricky glanced up just in time to see Bugsie and his gang laughing and flipping him the bird through the rear window.

He glared at the bus until it disappeared a few seconds later with the next twist in the road, then kicked at a stone and watched it skip across the tar, pretending it was Bugsie's head. "One of these days," he promised himself, "I'm gonna beat the crap out of that kid."

Lyle, who was cleaning off his glasses with the hem of his untucked T-shirt, added, "And one of these days Our Cop's gonna give Mr. Mack a ticket for driving so friggin' fast. Just hope I'm on the bus when he does."

"Scouts' Honor, his own mother won't know his face when I'm done with it." Ricky struck a boxer's stance and pummeled the air with his fists. "Take that! And that! You snot-sucking skid."

Having donned his glasses, Lyle jumped into the imaginary fray, throwing a punch at their invisible tormentor. "That's the last time he calls me Four-Eyes," he proclaimed, and they started laughing.

For a time, they chewed Bugsie up with brilliant

statements such as Lyle's: "Bugsie smells so bad he makes a wheelbarrow full of cow flaps smell like roses." But after two more bends in the road, their banter came to a sudden halt as both boys got a glimpse of the Beady property through the bare trees.

Ricky had been so preoccupied with the idea of keeping his deal with Mr. Daniels he'd forgotten that walking home included having to walk by . . .

"The Murder House," croaked Lyle.

Chapter Two

Roland Beady, like three generations of his family before him, had lived on Ridge Road his entire life. Some folks in Harmony Center said he'd lost his senses after his wife died; others said he'd always been a little odd. But everyone agreed that he was harmless, just a kindly old man who, despite the weather, had liked to sit by his mailbox and wave at people driving by. Although his daughter and son had repeatedly tried to talk him into living with one of them, he'd stubbornly refused to leave the house where he'd been born and raised. It was a big colonial that his great-grandfather built in 1842, and its clapboard siding was as gray as driftwood. To all the kids on Ridge Road, Roland Beady was a permanent landmark. They'd been as shocked as their parents when, the previous November, they'd heard "Wavin' Beady" had been murdered.

And now, as Ricky and Lyle stood and stared at the run-down house, Ricky felt the same shivering

15

sensation that had come over him whenever he'd been awakened in the middle of the night by his father's drunken voice, or the crash of furniture, or his mother's stifled screams. A tremor of fear that warned: *Danger!*

"The Murder House," Lyle croaked again, then threw a panicked look up and down the road as though hoping to see a car, or a neighbor out walking, or another way home. "Jesum-crow, Ricky. How'd you talk me into this?"

Although Ricky heard his friend's question, he couldn't pull himself away from the nightmare feeling that glued his feet to the ground. He just stood there gaping at the two huge oaks towering over the house, their network of branches reaching like hands above the front lawn where Wavin' Beady had been murdered. Even at that distance, he could see the remains of the ribbon the police had put up last fall, its red tattered plastic still attached in places to wooden stakes and flapping in the breeze like flags.

"Let's get out of here," whispered Lyle, his voice growing raspy. "This place gives me the creeps. It's like he's gonna walk out that front door any second and start waving at us."

"He's dead," said Ricky, but he wasn't just referring to Wavin' Beady. "When you're dead, you're dead." No matter what his father said in that awful dream Ricky kept having, he couldn't come back, couldn't hurt Ricky anymore. To prove it, Ricky took a step forward, then another, Lyle so close on his heels that he could hear the soft whistle of his friend's breathing.

Ricky hadn't been this close to the Beady place since the murder. He'd only rode by in the bus, where kids warned each other that the Murder House was coming so they could hold their breath, like they did when passing by cemeteries. Now he could see things he couldn't from the window of the bus—a torn yellowed shade in an upstairs window, an island of dirty snow by the stone foundation that hadn't yet melted. What he couldn't see was the big crow that was hidden in a cluster of roadside thistle, pecking at a dead squirrel.

Just as Lyle finished reminding him that the killer hadn't been caught yet, they neared the thistle, startling the crow away from its meal.

Ricky caught a glimpse of black wings, heard the angry *caw*, *caw*; the next thing he knew, he was sprinting by Wavin' Beady's driveway.

Lyle raced right beside him, but after a hundred yards or so, he could no longer keep up and collapsed in a wheezing heap on the side of the road. By the time Ricky noticed and ran back to him, Lyle was growing blue around the mouth and gasping for air.

With his heartbeat drumming in his ears, Ricky scanned the road for signs of help, but there was no one and no cars coming. He dropped to his knees and quickly patted his friend's pockets. "Where is it?" he demanded, panic starting to seize him, sweat already breaking out along the edges of his forehead.

Lyle pointed a shaky finger at his backpack.

Ricky yanked the zipper open and frantically searched through the bag until his fingers finally touched the small cylinder. "I've got it, Lyle! Just take it easy."

With trembling fingers, he flipped off the orange cap, shook up the yellow cylinder, then shoved the inhaler in his front pocket. Still on his knees, he scuttled around Lyle's heaving body so quickly that he almost lost his balance. Everything in the moment that it took to steady himself seemed magnified—the faded brown of the dead leaves, the terrifying sound of Lyle gulping for air, the faint smell of urine.

He positioned himself behind Lyle and shoved his hands beneath Lyle's armpits, feeling ribs and the hard flutter of breaths beneath his fingers. Struggling, he hoisted Lyle's rigid body to a semi-sitting position, just like he'd been taught, and then, using his legs and torso like the back of a chair, he held Lyle against him with one hand, and with the other held the inhaler to his friend's mouth. "All set?" he panted.

Lyle gave a slight nod.

Ricky depressed the inhaler, and Lyle took a puff of the powdery spray. "Hold it in!" Ricky ordered, then counted out loud to ten as though it were a comforting prayer. "Once more," said Ricky, and after Lyle complied, Ricky removed the inhaler and counted again. "That's it, Lyle," he coached, watching the rise and fall of his friend's chest. "Slow breath in, big breath out. Slow breath in, big breath out . . . ."

In the matter of a minute, the rigid shoulders beneath Ricky's sweaty palms began to feel more like rubber than rock, and he knew from experience that was a good sign. Already Lyle's color was coming back, his wheezing beginning to subside. "You're doing great," Ricky told him; resting his chin on top of Lyle's head, he let out a deep breath. No matter how many times he'd seen Lyle have asthma attacks, they still terrified him.

Normally they would have waited until Lyle could talk in sentences before walking again, but under the circumstances, even Lyle was willing to risk another attack rather than stay that close to Wavin' Beady's. As soon as he gasped, "Home," Ricky helped him to his feet.

Ricky took Lyle's backpack and they continued down the curvy road. He wasn't sure if Lyle's attack had been brought on by fear or by the running; either way, he felt responsible. He should have known better than to let Lyle walk home with him, should have remembered about the Murder House. He gave a tentative glance over his shoulder toward the place where Lyle had collapsed, a spot he could no longer see, and felt a sharp quiver of fear and guilt. What would have happened if Lyle had forgotten his inhaler? He turned his back on the scary thought, then reached out and touched Lyle's arm. "You okay?"

Lyle pushed up his glasses and sniffed. "I hate my asthma," he said, his voice still sounding froggy.

"You'll grow out of it," encouraged Ricky. "The

doctor said so." But as they walked along in silence, Ricky watched the tar beneath his feet for heaves, for pinpricks of glitter embedded by the winter sandings, for any reason not to look at his friend. After what they'd just been through, his encouragement had sounded like a lie.

The Benson farm interrupted the wooded terrain along Ridge Road for about a half a mile, allowing a clear view of the white house and huge red barn nestled in the shadow of Hatchet Mountain. When they reached the driveway, Lyle confessed something that Ricky already knew: "I wet my pants."

Ricky, who was drawing a circle in the dirt with the toe of his worn-out shoe, looked up at Lyle. "So?" he said. "At least you didn't throw up this time. 'Sides, I almost shit my draws when that friggin' crow jumped out at us."

For the first time since rounding that bend and laying eyes on the Beady place, both boys laughed.

"Think it could have been Wavin' Beady come back as a bird?" asked Lyle, taking off his jacket and tying it around his waist.

"Naw, he wasn't mean enough to come back as a crow," Ricky told him. He looked past Lyle, past the brown Jersey cows and the barnyard where Lyle's older brothers looked the size of dolls, until his gaze finally rested on the hardwoods that covered Hatchet Mountain. "A tree, maybe," he said, "so he could still wave at people."

"Yeah," said Lyle, nodding his head as though the idea pleased him. "A maple tree—they wave the best."

One of the cows let out a bawl, and both boys looked in its direction. "I better get changed before my mother finds out," said Lyle, tugging at the jacket around his waist. "It'll be worse than missing chores if she knows why I had an attack. She don't want me near that place, not even with my big brothers."

"You'd better not walk home with me again then," said Ricky, latching on to the good excuse that could, without hurting Lyle's feelings, replace the real truth—he didn't want Lyle to have another attack, didn't want to be forced to walk instead of run by the Murder House, didn't want to have to choose between his deal with Mr. Daniels and his best friend. "Wouldn't want her to be mad at me, or for you to get in trouble."

The good excuse seemed to relieve Lyle, too. "Yeah," he agreed eagerly, "I better not."

"I'll see you tomorrow," said Ricky, handing Lyle his backpack. "Don't bother to save me a seat on the bus, 'cause I'll be walking."

"I'll save it for Matt then," Lyle told him with a devilish smile. "Scouts' Honor, Bugsie gives him any trouble—I'll fix him. I'll pretend to have an attack, then blame it on him. That will get Bugsie's butt in enough trouble to leave your little brother alone."

Ricky started laughing. "Good thinking. Be a lot easier walking if I know I don't have to worry about Matt. Thanks, Lyle."

"What are best friends for?" asked Lyle, but he didn't wait for an answer; he turned and started down the driveway, his jacket still secured around his thin waist, its sleeves wagging at his sides with each step.

Watching him walk away, Ricky found himself wanting to help Lyle, too, wishing that somehow he could make the asthma just disappear. With a sigh, he turned and looked at the long road ahead of him, gauging in his mind how long it would take him to walk the last mile alone.

...Chapter Three

When Ricky finally made it home, his little brother and their dog, Boomer, were waiting for him at the end of the driveway. "They all called you chicken for walking," Matt reported.

Ricky looked at his little brother. With his blue eyes and blond hair, Matt didn't look like a Gordon at all, and because of that their father used to say, *He ain't no kid of mine.* He said it so often, Matt had gone around telling his friends he'd been adopted. "Bugsie didn't bother you on the bus, did he?" Ricky asked with concern.

Matt chucked a stick, and Boomer, who was half coon dog and half mutt, raced after it. "Nah," said Matt, "he'd look like a wuss if he started pickin' on a second-grader. 'Sides, I can take care of myself."

"Just stay away from him," Ricky warned, but he could tell Matt wasn't listening. He had that faraway look in his eyes, a sort of blank stare that sometimes came over him. It used to really bug their father, who'd tell Matt, *Stop your star dazing or I'll give you something to wake you up.*

"Hit him with that fry pan that time, didn't I?" said Matt wistfully. "Knocked him right out."

From the time they were little, Ricky and Matt had always referred to their father as "him" or "he" or "the old man," but never Dad. "Yeah, you did," said Ricky, remembering that night. His mother on the floor trying to protect her face, his father's boots kicking at her arms, him in the middle trying to break it up, and then Matt coming out of nowhere, swinging a cast-iron fry pan. "And you were just lucky he was too drunk to remember."

"I wanted him to remember," snapped Matt.

Ricky looked at his brother—the blank stare was gone; the blue eyes now flashed with anger. That woke him up, thought Ricky, but to Matt he said, "Don't get mad at me."

"If Ma hadn't made us promise to keep it a secret I would have told him."

There was no doubt in Ricky's mind that Matt would have. Their father had always blamed him for asking for it. Although Matt was terrified of their father, he couldn't stop himself from talking back. Ricky had always admired his little brother for that, but had hated him for it, too; it just made things worse in the end. He'd no sooner get things calmed down than Matt would open his mouth and it would start all over again. The thing was, now that their father was dead, Matt seemed more scared of him than when he was alive.

"He probably knows about it now, anyhow," said Matt, looking worried. "The devil probably told him all about it when he got to hell."

Ricky laughed, then looked through leafless trees at their two-bedroom shack. The translucent plastic that covered the two front windows was starting to come apart at the edges. His father had stapled on the plastic every fall; called it a "thrifty man's storm window." Ricky hated the way it fogged the windows from the inside so you couldn't see out.

"Probably told him about the time I spit on his eggs, too," Matt continued as they headed toward the small yard filled with dead tires, thawing dog mess, and junk. They passed by an old bathroom sink that was mired in the muddy ground near a stack of cordwood. Then they dodged around the rusty Ford truck that was propped up on blocks and still waiting, after three years, for an engine.

When they reached the porch, Matt hung back as usual. "You go first," he said.

Ricky always had to walk in the house first, to make sure for Matt that their father hadn't somehow risen from the dead and come home. After pretending to check the rooms inside, Ricky stuck his head out the front door and informed Matt, who was still standing on the bottom step, "He ain't here."

"Did you check the bathroom, too?" asked Matt.

Ricky rolled his eyes skyward. He was getting tired

of having to do this every day. "Yeah, I checked the bathroom."

Matt studied the front door a moment more. "Just wish Ma would hurry up and get him buried. Don't know what those cemetery people are waiting for, the ground ain't frozen anymore."

Their father had died in January, when the ground was rock-solid and too deep with snow for the cemetery workers to dig a grave. The knowledge that his body was still sitting in the cemetery's winter vault instead of in the ground bothered Ricky, too. He worried about it in ways he'd never tell Matt, who was scared enough. He'd just keep checking the house for their dead father for as long as Matt needed him to do it. "Come on," he said gently. "I'll cook us some Spaghetti-O's."

· · ■ · ·

When their mother and Katie came home, Ricky and Matt were on the couch watching TV. "Hurry up, Ma," said Matt, "Oprah's got a lady on who can talk to dead people."

Even before his mother said, "Shut the TV off," Ricky could tell he was in trouble, just by the look she was giving him.

As though he could read that look, too, Matt shut off the TV without protest, then scooped up his baby sister and beat it outside.

After the door closed, Ricky's mother sat down on the couch beside him and kicked off her shoes. Ricky continued to stare at the color TV perched on an apple crate like a holy statue. When their father was alive, they weren't allowed to touch it. It was *his,* bought with *his* insurance money that he'd gotten for hurting *his* back. After Katie learned to crawl and climb, it was a constant battle to keep her away from it. Now she wouldn't go near it. Ricky figured it was because she still remembered the one time she'd touched the vertical-hold knob. Their father had backhanded her right across the face, swatting her away like she was nothing more than a fly.

"So," his mother finally said, "I heard you had some trouble at school today."

Can't even fart in this town without everybody knowing it, thought Ricky. "Who told you?"

"Cindy overheard her kids talking when they got home from school. She made them tell me the whole story, so don't be giving them any grief for it."

"Did they tell you what Bugsie said?"

"It was a mean thing to say, and I don't blame you for wanting to hit him. But that doesn't make it right."

He looked at his new mother, wondering where the old one had gone. The one who used to cry in the middle of the night when she thought no one was listening. The one who kept his secrets. Was she still in there somewhere? Did she still hear *his* footsteps in her dreams, hear the sound of the belt whistling through loopholes? "What was I supposed to do, Ma? Just stand there while he said that crap in front of Matt?"

"Watch your mouth."

Ricky jumped up and started to pace the small room, feeling the urge to kick *his* TV right through the window. Why hadn't this new mother been there to tell *him* to watch *his* mouth? Every other word the "F" one. Saying those things that hurt worse than the belt and black eyes. *The sorriest day of my life was the day you were born.*

Where was she then? Ricky turned and looked at her, his eyes tracing the scar above her lip, the crooked nose, the droopy left eye, all caused by his father's fists. All reminders that she had tried. "Sorry, Ma. I didn't mean to make trouble for you. . . . You won't call Mr. McCarthy, will you?"

"The boy's just repeating what he's heard at home. Don't see it would do any good to talk to his father, do you?"

"No," said Ricky, and, feeling some relief, he flopped down on the couch beside her. His mother's arm came around him, and though part of him wanted to shake her off, he gave in to the comfort, the rest of his anger dissolving, for the moment, under her touch.

"You got a right to be angry, Ricky. All the things he did to you. To all of us. He's been dead two months now and I'm just waking up to it."

Exactly sixty days today, thought Ricky. His father's truck had been discovered by Our Cop at 2:00 A.M. on New Year's Day.

"That's why I think it's time we saw Dr. Munsen again. Maybe we weren't ready to talk to her before."

Just hearing that name was enough to set Ricky off,

and he angrily pushed his mother's arm away. There was no way he was going back to that place.

"It means filling out all that paperwork again," his mother continued. "But I need to talk to someone. Need to get Matt some help for his nightmares. . . ."

He'd hated her office—the rich furniture, all those smiling pictures of her husband and kids, the magazine-looking people in her waiting room. He'd felt dirty just sitting there. It was Aunt Donna who had put that idea in his mother's head—no wonder his father never let her come over when he was alive! Dragging them all the way up to Bangor, telling his mother the whole way how lucky they were Dr. Munsen had said she'd see them for free because she was writing some book. Aunt Donna going on and on about it like they were on their way to see someone more famous than God. The only reason he'd agreed to go in the first place was his aunt's promise to take them to McDonald's, but, like Matt had said as soon as they'd gotten out of the car, "There ain't no Happy Meal worth listening to that."

From the second they'd walked into that fancy office it was like a bad dream. Katie, with a load in her pants, howling because her bottle was empty; Matt opening every door in the place looking for a bathroom; his mother standing there in the summer jacket she wore for a winter coat, trying to explain to the lady behind the desk that they had an appointment. Then Aunt Donna charging through the door, complaining about the parking, her pocketbook that was the size of a suitcase bumping against a lady's chair and knocking her fur hat on the floor, and him having to pick it up 'cause his aunt couldn't bend over that far.

It was awful.

Some of the people in the waiting room were too polite to stare, others looked like they were afraid they might catch something from them—a cold or bugs or being poor, Ricky wasn't sure what. And Aunt Donna doing her best to make friends with all of them, saying nice things about their clothes, about the flowers and the pictures on the walls. Them waiting there forever just to see a doctor for free; a lady who was so nice he didn't trust her. He hadn't answered one of her questions. Neither had Matt nor their mother. The only ones who ended up talking were Dr. Munsen and Aunt Donna. They'd yapped for almost an hour, but the only thing Ricky remembered was his aunt saying, "His death was a blessing in disguise."

"I ain't going back there," Ricky now told his mother. "Even if Aunt Donna promised to take us to Disney World I wouldn't go."

"I know it was hard for you," said his mother, who was staring at the TV like she was watching something on its empty screen. "It was hard for me, too. He made me a secret keeper before I even married him, and then, suddenly, he's dead and I'm supposed to tell it all to some woman I just said hello to. No explaining that to your Aunt Donna. She'll stop a stranger on the street and tell them her life story."

His mother let out a defeated sigh that seemed to shake her whole body. "But I'm at the end of my rope here," she said in a voice barely above a whisper. "I've tried everything I can think of to help Matt get over those bad dreams and they're only getting worse. Waking up to those screams every night, and him wetting the bed; now he won't even go to sleep unless he has that fry pan with him." She paused for just a second, and in a firmer voice said, "If Dr. Munsen can help him, I'll tell her anything she wants to know."

His mother turned and looked at him as though she'd forgotten he was there. "Don't mind me," she told him. "I'm just thinking out loud." Then she cupped his chin with the palm of her hand and studied his lip. "It kills me you kids are still paying for his sins. Maybe I *should* call up that boy's father."

Ricky lifted his chin out of his mother's hand. "Bugsie's my problem. You've got enough to worry about." Matt, Katie's ear infections, bills, that junker of a car that wouldn't start half the time. "I can handle this myself, Ma. Just let me."

His mother gave him a long look, as though trying to make a decision. "Okay," she finally said. "But if that boy touches you again, I'll be down to that school in a heartbeat. Understand? No one hits my kids.... Not anymore."

··■··

"He's coming! He's coming! No, no . . . don't . . ."

"Wake up, Matt." Ricky shook his brother's shoulder. "It's only a dream; he ain't coming."

Matt jerked away from him and let out a blood-curdling scream, and Boomer, who was sleeping under Katie's crib in their mother's room, started growling.

Ricky shook his brother again, this time more roughly. "If you wet our bed again, I'm gonna kill you myself. Now, wake up!"

In the dimness of the Jesus night-light, Ricky watched his brother's shadowy face rolling back and forth on the pillow. He could feel Matt's legs twitching beneath the covers, could sense the next scream coming, and covered his brother's mouth with his hand. "Be quiet," he said, as Matt moaned against his palm. "You're going to wake up the whole house."

But most everyone was already awake—Boomer, Ricky, and now his mother, whose hurried footsteps he could hear coming down the hall. The overhead light, whose globe had been broken during a fight and had never been replaced, flashed on, and Ricky let go of Matt's mouth to shield his eyes against the blinding glare of the naked bulb.

"Hurry," said his mother, her hands already reaching for Matt. "Help me get him to the bathroom."

"Too late for that," Ricky told her, then flipped back the covers, exposing the evidence and the cast-iron fry pan lying beside his sleeping brother.

"He got the blanket, too," his mother sighed.

Ricky yawned, and for a moment he just sat there on the far edge of the bed, still groggy with sleep and too weary to move. "I can't take this anymore," he said, then looked away from them. He stared at the wall, whose beige paint was soot-colored along the ceiling from years of heating the house with wood, then lowered his gaze to the collage of pictures cut out of *National Geographics* that he and Matt had salvaged from the town dump and taped to the wall—Mount Everest, Kodiak Island, the green Amazon jungle— and, below them, a small printed message he'd written himself: *Anywhere but Here.*

"You never should have let him watch that stupid show," he heard his mother say.

That thought had crossed Ricky's mind, but he'd been too interested in the lady who could see and talk to the dead to change the station. He'd wanted to call her up on the phone and ask her if, while she was at it, could she tell his father—William, Willy Gordon—to rot in hell. But right now he was too angry at his brother for wetting their bed again, and too irritated by his mother's tone, to admit that what she said was true. "It's all my fault, right?" he asked sarcastically.

"You should have known better," she scolded.

"Well, maybe if you'd get *him* buried, Matt'd stop doing this. Ever think of that?"

"I'm not going to stand here at two-thirty in the morning and have a blaming match with you, Ricky. Now, get over here and help me so we can get back to bed."

He turned and looked at his mother, whose new haircut still took him by surprise, but whose thin, tired face he recognized. Her eyes were now pleading with him. "I'm coming," he told her.

He helped her strip Matt out of his wet T-shirt and skivvies, and Matt woke up enough to ask, "Again?"

"Don't worry, sweetie," said their mother, brushing back his sweaty bangs. "It's okay. You come with me, now. I'll get you washed up, then you can sleep in my room."

Ricky watched his mother guide Matt, who was still half asleep and naked, out the door. "I'll get the Lysol," he told her, now resigned to the work ahead. Like having to check the house for their dead father, Matt's bedwetting had become a routine, too. While his mother got Matt cleaned up and settled, Ricky would strip the bed, wash the plastic mattress-cover down with Lysol, then collect the bedding and wet clothes and take them out to the washer. Because their dryer had been dead longer than their father, his mother wouldn't go back to sleep until the wash was hanging on the line by the woodstove. With the blanket, Ricky knew that meant two loads tonight instead of one.

He looked down at the bed, at the fry pan that had replaced his little brother's stuffed bear. Even dead, thought Ricky, he still gets us.

...Chapter Four

Although he'd scrubbed his hands with soap, Ricky could still smell the Lysol as he watched his mother from his bed on the couch. If it weren't a school night she'd let him keep her company and help hang the wash, like he usually did on the weekends. Even though she was sitting with her back to him, he could see the coffee cup by her wrist and the edges of the green folder that she kept the bills in. Over the thumping heartbeat of the washing machine, he heard her say "Jesus" as she looked through the bills they never had enough money to pay. Just by the way her back was all humped over, he knew she was as tired as he was. He felt sorry for her and guilty for wanting, more than anything, just to close his eyes and go to sleep while she was still out there working.

When Ricky woke up at five-thirty and looked toward the kitchen, the light was off and his mother was gone. He rubbed at the crust in the corners of his eyes, then pulled the thin blanket up around his shoulders. Although it wasn't officially spring yet according to the calendar, it was already growing lighter earlier in the mornings, and even through the fog of plastic covering the windows he could make out the furniture in the room and the dark outline of *his* TV. If I'm here, he thought, Matt must have wet the bed. Then last night came back to him, as well as Lyle's asthma attack, and the crow flying up at them through those bushes. He remembered the Murder House and the reason why he and Lyle had been near enough to see that torn shade in the window. "Friggin' Bugsie," he muttered.

Still weak from lack of sleep, Ricky didn't want to move. For a while he struggled with his conscience—his mother already knew about the fight with Bugsie, so why bother to keep his deal with Mr. Daniels? He could just go back to sleep for another hour and ride the bus to school with Matt. But then thoughts of his mother crept in, and he remembered the guilt and sorrow he'd felt watching her sit at the kitchen table just a few hours before. She didn't need his worries piled on that hunched back. Besides, yesterday, right here in this room, he'd promised her he could handle his problem with Bugsie. Get moving, he told himself, you have to walk to school. He figured if he left early enough he wouldn't have to watch the bus pass him, and it was that idea that finally lifted him off the couch.

·· ■ ··

It was chilly out, the ground wet with frosty dew, the sun barely crowning the treetops, a sliver of moon still left in the sky. As he walked toward the Lewises', he heard the first robins of spring singing in the village of birdhouses that Mr. Lewis had built for his wife. The Lewises were an old couple who'd never had any children until Ricky had stolen his way into their lives.

He stopped to watch a robin perched on a furrow in the vegetable garden that wouldn't be planted until late May. The bird's head was bent, twisted parallel to the ground, as it patiently listened for worms. This reminded Ricky of the day he'd been crawling on his belly through that garden looking for something to eat, too. He was only five, and that morning had been a bad one at his house—his father drinking and on the warpath with his belt. Ricky had escaped through the bedroom window, then taken off for the woods. He'd walked around for hours, playing and exploring, and by the time he'd wandered onto the Lewises' property he was hungry enough to eat dirt. He'd found something better—rhubarb. It wasn't the first time he'd raided their garden, but it was the first time he'd gotten caught. He was chomping away on one sour stalk and grabbing for more to add to his pile when a hand grabbed him by the scruff of the neck. He'd scraped his knee in the struggle to get away, but Mr. Lewis had a good hold on him and wouldn't let go. He'd marched Ricky right into their kitchen, where Mrs. Lewis was baking cookies, and told her, "I won't have to bait that trap anymore, Martha. Here's our raccoon."

Ricky had figured he was in big trouble, but Mrs. Lewis started yelling at her husband instead of him. He'd stood there between them, bewildered; he didn't think that was something a wife was supposed to do. He was afraid Mr. Lewis might beat her right in front of him, yet Mrs. Lewis didn't seem afraid at all. "You're worse than Mr. McGregor in *Peter Rabbit*," she'd scolded him, like her husband was a little kid or something. It made Ricky wonder if she was crazy like his Aunt June the Loon, who'd cuss at anybody and liked to bark like a dog. But if she was crazy, Ricky didn't mind, because, the next thing he knew, she was feeding him cinnamon-oatmeal cookies at the kitchen table and fussing over his knee. It was nothing more than a scrape, but she'd cleaned it all up and put a Band-Aid on it. He could still remember how pink her scalp was beneath her thin white hair as she'd knelt before him washing his leg, could see vividly those wrinkled hands with their wormlike veins touching his dirty skin so tenderly.

He looked away from the garden, feeling a sadness so deep it made his eyes water. He missed Mrs. Lewis. Those blue eyes had always looked at him as though he were a Christmas present. Whenever he'd finished mowing the lawn or stacking wood, Mrs. Lewis used to tell him what a good job he'd done. She'd call him a hard worker, a smart boy. She was so nice that the birds used to eat right out of her hand—even blue jays, and they never trusted anyone. No matter what kind of trouble he'd gotten into at school or in town, she'd always found a good excuse for it. Never once had she said anything about the little things he took from her house—pencils, pens, spare change—little thefts that eventually shamed him and changed his understanding of right and wrong. Although he knew it wasn't her fault, there was a part of him that was still mad at her for dying last spring.

Trying to shake those sad thoughts from his mind, he looked at the house. The blinds were closed, and Mr. Lewis' car was still in the driveway. Mr. Lewis owned the lumber mill next to the general store, and even though he was going on eighty and had already had a heart attack, he got up every morning and went to work six days out of seven. Some people said he was the richest man in Harmony Center, but Ricky wasn't sure if that was true, because Mr. Lewis still drove a car that was two years older than Ricky was, and in the winter he closed off all the rooms in his house except for a couple, so it wouldn't cost him "an arm and a leg" to heat the place. Although Ricky still mowed his lawn in the summer, shoveled his driveway in the winter, and worked for him on Saturday mornings at the mill doing scut work, Mr. Lewis never told him he did a good job. He just paid Ricky three dollars an hour, fed him while he was there, and was always quick to point out anything he did wrong.

Ricky shifted the weight in his backpack and hurried on past the driveway, the birdhouses, and the barn where he and Matt had slept a handful of times when their house was too dangerous. The two of them used to hide in the woods until it was dark enough to sneak into the barn unnoticed. Then they'd huddle under the blue tarp, listening for the sound of drunken footsteps above the whine of hungry mosquitoes, and the night noises of crickets, peepers, and hoot owls. The fear that *he* might have followed them or figured out where they'd gone had always kept them from any real sleep while they'd waited for morning.

As Ricky relived that memory, the sound of his own footsteps on the roadside gravel was muffled by the voice of his little brother pleading with him in the dark.

"Can't we *please* get a drink of water, Ricky? I ain't got no more spit left to swallow."

"No, I told you, we might get caught."

"But Mr. Lewis is half deaf. He'll never hear us turn on the hose."

Matt had begged and begged until Ricky had finally given in to him and his own torturous thirst. Holding hands, they'd sprinted through the darkness across the dew-slick grass, both willing to risk being caught just for a mouthful of water. He could still remember the deafening sound of the well's pump kicking in when he turned the spigot, and how they'd gulped that rubbery-tasting water until their bellies were so full they swished with it when they ran back to the barn.

Inside, Ricky could feel the anger rising. No matter where he went in this town, there were always reminders. Whether it was a robin hunting worms or a quick glance at a barn, there was no getting away from *him*. One of these days he was going to hop on one of those trains that passed along the steel trestle up by Dead Man's Curve and ride out of this town for good. Leave it behind like a bad dream and go someplace where there were no reminders, where no one knew him or said his last name like a swear word. Somewhere like one of those places on his bedroom wall. The only hope he'd ever dared to own was *Anywhere but Here*.

When he walked by the Bensons', all the lights were on in the barn, and he figured Lyle was probably in there with his father and brothers doing the morning milking. Whenever someone at school made fun of Lyle for stinking like cows, Lyle would tell them, "That's the smell of money." Lyle was always saying funny things like that, and now, as Ricky passed by his friend's house, it made him wish Lyle was walking with him. He wished this even more as he drew nearer to the Murder House.

Before Wavin' Beady was killed, Ricky had never been afraid of walking anywhere in Harmony Center. In fact, summer days were mostly spent wandering— building forts with Matt in the woods up on Hatchet Mountain, fishing and swimming down on Loon Lake. Sometimes they'd take the baby carriage and go bottle hunting along the back roads to collect enough for Italian sandwiches and ice creams down at the general store. Sometimes they'd hike all the way to Dead Man's Curve just for the chance to flatten a penny on the tracks when the train went by. Never once in all that venturing had he felt there was something to be afraid of other than the usual dangers that came with exploring—like the possibility of starting a forest fire while cooking up a can of beans in the woods, or maybe letting go of the Tarzan swing too early and landing on the rocks instead of in the lake.

But now whenever he was out in the woods he had the feeling that someone was hiding behind a tree or a rock just waiting to kill him. If truth be told, he was scared to walk down his own road alone, and he wished again that Lyle were with him.

Even before he rounded the bend that led past the place where Wavin' Beady's daughter had found her father's battered body, Ricky was sprinting. Although he was badly winded, he didn't stop running until he'd made it all the way to Slowpoke Clara's.

By the time he got to the Bakers' farm pond, the morning traffic was starting. Mr. Lafayette, on his way home from his night watch at the mill, was the first to drive by. Ricky noticed that when the drivers caught sight of him they slowed down abruptly, as though he were a pothole in the road they hadn't expected. But no one stopped to ask why he was walking or if he wanted a ride, and he was grateful no one did.

He left Ridge Road, crossed Route 26, and followed that for a quarter of a mile before cutting into the quiet, wet woods. At the initial tree, he hesitated just long enough to run his eyes over the plus sign that joined his parents' initials and the inscription carved below—*4-ever*. He was just a little kid the first time he'd seen it, three going on four—old enough to remember his first black eye. He'd been rolling a baseball on the living-room floor and accidentally tipped over a beer bottle. His father, drunk and mad, had fired the ball back at him. The next morning, after his father had sobered up enough to remember what he'd done, he'd taken Ricky out for a ride. They'd gone up to the school yard, and while Ricky played on the swings and slide, his father had told him he was sorry he'd hit him, then made him promise he wouldn't tell anyone. He'd said that if Ricky did the police would come and take him away and he'd never get to see his mother or new baby brother again. Then he'd made him practice what he'd say if anyone asked: "I fell off the slide." Before they'd gone home, his father had taken him into the woods to show him the tree he'd carved up with a buck knife in sixth grade.

When he reached the fringe of the woods that led to the playground and Mr. Daniels' premises, Ricky noticed that none of the school buses had arrived yet, and that there were only a few cars in the teachers' parking lot. He'd never been early for school before. For a moment he stood there listening to his empty stomach rumble and debated whether he should wait in the woods until the buses started coming or if he should just go inside. Either way, he figured he might get in trouble. If Mr. Daniels caught him in the hall, he'd probably end up in the office for being too early. On the other hand, if he waited for the buses, chances were he'd run into Bugsie and walking to school would all be for nothing if they got into it. He decided to take his chances with Mr. Daniels.

Inside the school, voices, laughter, and the smell of toast spilled out of the teachers' coffee room and into the empty hallway. Down in the gym, which doubled as the school's cafeteria, he could hear the kitchen ladies banging pans and setting up the tables for the "Breakfast Eaters"—poor kids like him who could get their breakfast for free. When he was Matt's age and younger, it was something about school he'd always looked forward to—getting there in the morning and having oatmeal and fruit, or, on Wednesdays, scrambled eggs. It wasn't until the middle of last year that he'd come to realize that going hungry was easier to live with than being called a Breakfast Eater by his classmates.

Feeling like a trespasser, he carefully crept along the darkened hallways until he reached his classroom. His homeroom teacher, Mrs. Parker, whom he had for all his classes except math, was always late in the morning because she lived in Camden. Usually she didn't rush into the room until morning announcements on the intercom. Thus, after noting the time, he went right to his desk without fear of being discovered and began working on some math. When the buses started arriving, he was concentrating so hard on solving a percentage problem involving compound interest that he didn't even hear them drive up. It wasn't until Lyle tapped him on the back that he looked up and remembered where he was.

"How was walking?" asked Lyle.

Ricky shrugged. "Okay. Did you get in trouble yesterday?"

"Not bad," he said, sitting down at the desk beside Ricky's, "but of course she said I can't walk home with you anymore."

From the way Lyle was looking down at his shoes, Ricky had the feeling that wasn't all she had said. It was clear to him that most mothers in Harmony Center didn't want their sons hanging around a Gordon. Ricky had come to this realization long ago, but it was still especially painful when it came to Lyle's mother. Though Ricky couldn't help who his father was, or that his two uncles were living in Thomaston Prison, or that his Aunt June the Loon roamed the streets of Belfast now that the state had gotten rid of the mental hospital in Augusta, he'd always had the feeling that Mrs. Benson held his family against him. She was always nice enough; it was just the looks she'd sometimes give him, like whatever he was saying had to be a lie, and that feeling that she was always waiting for him to go home as soon as he knocked on their door. Still, he liked going to their house, liked pretending he was part of their family as he listened to the noise and joking that went on at the big kitchen table Lyle's father had built himself so that all nine Bensons could eat at the same time. Theirs was the kind of fighting that made everybody laugh.

There goes Lyle's house for a while, Ricky now thought.

"You know how she is," said Lyle apologetically. "But she'll get over it. By next week you'll be able to come over again."

"I suppose she gave you grief about Scouts again, too," said Ricky.

"Are you kidding? I'll be hearing about that till I'm fifty. Especially now that my brother Tim's gonna be a friggin' Eagle. But, hey, ask me if I care." Lyle pushed up his glasses and gave him a cocky smile. "I don't need no badge to know how to make a square knot. Anyhow, that's the least of our worries—Bugsie was looking for you on the bus. Seems his old man ran into Mr. Daniels down at the store last night, and Bugsie got grounded 'cause of it. He's ready to plow you into next Tuesday. And you gotta talk to Matt. His mouth's gonna get him in trouble, Ricky. He don't know when to shut up. I was sitting next to him on the bus, like I told you I would. Anyhow, Bugsie was up back bragging to his boys about you being so scared you had to walk, and Matt turns right around in his seat and yells down the aisle, 'Hey Bugsie, you smart enough to read sign language?' Then he gives him the finger and says, 'Read this!' "

Ricky started laughing, but it was short-lived. "Did he really?" he asked, with a sinking feeling.

"Scouts' Honor," said Lyle. "Thought Mr. Mack would give him a bus slip for sure, but he just kept on driving like he hadn't heard a thing. Just said, 'Keep it down,' when everybody started laughing."

"What'd Bugsie do?"

46

"What could he do?" said Lyle. "He can't go and hit a second-grader. He'll just save it up for you. Or maybe me, for sitting next to him."

"Don't worry, I'll talk to Matt," said Ricky. "I'll set him straight about it." But secretly he wondered if that was possible. He'd never been able to keep Matt from mouthing off to their father. Even in the middle of getting the belt, Matt would sometimes keep yelling stuff.

Just then, Mr. Daniels' voice boomed over the intercom with the morning announcements, and Mrs. Parker rushed through the door with her bags and coffee.

"Jesum-crow," Lyle whispered, "someone should give her a late slip."

But Ricky didn't hear him; he was still thinking about Matt.

.. ■ ..

As he'd promised Mr. Daniels, Ricky stayed in at recess, and while all the other kids were out on the playground hooting and hollering and having a good time, he studied the school calendar and did some figuring. There were 104 days until summer vacation. Minus Saturdays and Sundays, and April vacation, and the Monday holiday on Memorial Day weekend, that made a total of sixty-eight school days. Sixty-eight more times he would have to sit here while the others played outside. And, including yesterday and today, he would walk the distance between home and school 139 times. At an estimated distance of three and a half miles, that equaled ... Holy shit, thought Ricky, that's 486.5 miles! The wonderment of that figure hardly set in before his mind raced in another direction. According to his classroom clock, it had taken him sixty-three minutes to get there this morning; multiply that by 139 and divide that figure by 60—approximately 146 hours or six whole days of walking while that skid Bugsie rode the bus.

·· ■ ··

On his way home from school that afternoon, just as he sprinted past Wavin' Beady's, the bus passed him, and again Ricky had to watch Bugsie and his gang point, laugh, wave, and flip him the bird through the back window. And that's when it first came to him—the idea of beating the bus home.

The bus left school at 2:55 and arrived at his house about 3:20, give or take a few minutes. The time it had taken him minus the time it took the bus was thirty-eight minutes, thirty-nine to play it safe. I'd have to run the whole way to cut down that much time, thought Ricky. Looking down the road toward Wavin' Beady's, he wondered what the odds of doing that were.

As he ambled down the road, those odds began to consume him. He knelt down on the sandy shoulder and, using his finger for a pencil, did some figuring in the dirt. He became so deeply engrossed in the factors of distance and speed that he probably would have stayed there a lot longer if Slowpoke Clara hadn't come along on her bike.

Seeing Ricky kneeling there, scratching in the dirt, she stopped to ask, "What'd you lose, Ricky?"

Slowpoke Clara was in his class, and though she couldn't even do division, she was nice to look at. She had straw-colored hair and blue eyes and was the only girl in fifth grade that needed to wear a bra. "Nothing," he told her, then quickly erased his work in the sand, the tips of his ears feeling like they were on fire.

Clara raised one pretty eyebrow at him. "Oh," she said. "I'll see ya, then. I'm late, have to meet . . . someone."

Ricky watched her pedal away, her golden pigtails bouncing slightly and flashing in the sun. Slowly, he stood up, his knees feeling knotted from kneeling so long. I should have told her I lost my mind, he thought, glancing down at the work he'd covered up in the sand, one part of a 5 still visible. Unlike Matt, he could never think of a wisecrack or anything clever to say until it was too late. The only thing he'd thought of when she was standing there asking if he'd lost something was "Too bad I don't have a bike." If he had, making those numbers in the sand work wouldn't be difficult at all.

Chapter Five

Ricky knew he wouldn't be able to run the distance before he could jog it. Each morning he set a new goal for himself: jog to the Denisons' without stopping, jog to the Bensons', the Hatchet Mountain sign, the Williamses', the Bakers' farm pond, and so forth. In the afternoon he reversed the order.

The first few days were the hardest. He got blisters on the back of his heels from his Goodwill shoes, and even with Bag Balm and Band-Aids, his feet hurt. He was sore and stiff—not just his legs but his whole body. As he explained to Matt, "It feels like the time the old man cornered me in the living room and beat me with the mop handle."

Despite his sore muscles and tender feet, each day Ricky managed to jog a little farther. He started padding his shoes, which were a half-size too big, with toilet paper. He learned that, if he didn't dwell on his blisters, or the cramp in his side, or the burning in his lungs, it didn't hurt as much. To take his mind off these things, he played number games in his head: counting telephone poles, adding up the road numbers on mailboxes, converting speed signs from miles to kilometers. Sometimes he recited units of distance he knew by rote: 5,280 feet = 1,760 yards = 320 rods = 80 chains = 1 mile. Other times he made up problems to solve: If Mr. Lewis gave me a 2-percent raise, how much extra money would I make after working 15 hours? If I put $5 a week in the bank at 5 percent simple interest, how much money would I have at the end of the year? If I had 19 fights with Bugsie and lost 3 of them, what percentage of those fights did I win?

It took Ricky seventeen days to be able to jog all the way to school without stopping, and during those thirty-four times of trying, things had been happening. The blisters on his heels turned into calluses, the muscles in his legs grew stronger, the books in his backpack seemed lighter. He discovered that if he breathed in through his mouth and exhaled through his nose he didn't get as many cramps. He learned that it was easier to make it up the big hills if he leaned forward, took shorter steps, and pumped his arms harder.

He observed other things as well. On sunny mornings, Mrs. Denison sat on her back-door steps in a blue bathrobe drinking coffee, and on foggy mornings deer came to the edges of the open field by Hatchet Mountain. He noticed that Mr. Lafayette and other morning drivers began to wave and honk when they passed him on the road, and that the Williamses' dog,

Sage, now waited at the end of their driveway as though he knew just when Ricky was supposed to come by and pat him.

In the afternoons, Tom Guimond had a habit of barreling down Ridge Road on his flashy red mountain bike. Although Tom was a seventh-grader and one of the popular kids that hung out by the general store, he'd always been nice to Ricky if none of his friends were around. Tom's father worked for Mr. Lewis in the mill, and a few times on Saturday mornings he'd brought his son in to do scut jobs. It was over those tasks of sorting knotted wood and sweeping and such that Ricky had come to know Tom enough to say "Hi" when they met on the road.

For a while, Ricky just assumed Tom headed for the store to hang out with his friends, but then, one day when he'd stayed after school to work on a difficult math problem with Mr. Garvey, Ricky spotted Tom's red bike in the bushes just past the Bensons', and Slowpoke Clara's blue one was resting right beside it. It wasn't hard for him to figure out that the "someone" Clara was on her way to meet that day he'd been kneeling by the side of the road was Tom. But, like the rest of the things he had noticed of late, it was something he kept to himself.

Still, there were some things that hadn't changed since the first day he'd walked home with Lyle. He still sprinted by Wavin' Beady's no matter how tired he was, and every afternoon the bus still passed by with Bugsie and his gang in the back seat yelling things out the window. And except for Tuesdays, when Matt had his appointments with Dr. Munsen, his little brother and Boomer were always waiting for him by the mailbox at the end of their driveway. So, when he didn't see Matt or their dog sitting by the mailbox one Friday afternoon, Ricky was alarmed.

Certain that something bad had happened, Ricky broke into a run, his mind trying to make sense of his brother's absence. Maybe Ma didn't go to work. Maybe Matt was just peeing in the bushes. But as Ricky sprinted down the driveway, his fear only grew as he looked through the trees whose leaves hadn't yet begun to bud—there was no car, and no sign of Matt or Boomer.

Cutting across the yard to save time, he hurdled over dead tires and broken toys, his shoes barely touching the ground. "Matt! Matt!" he yelled.

In those few seconds his mind raced even faster than his legs, the threat he'd made to his little brother cutting into his guilty heart like a knife—*If I ever hear of you giving Bugsie lip again, I'll tell all your friends you sleep with a fry pan and wet the bed every night.*

He took the three steps of their porch in one leap, his hand already reaching for the door. But just as he grabbed for the knob, the door swung outward, the metal handle striking his knuckles. A frightened yelp came up his throat and out of his mouth. He jumped backward, shaking his injured hand to get rid of the needling pain in his fingers.

"What's the matter?" asked Matt, who was standing

in the doorway chewing on a saltine. "The Flying Monkeys after you?"

Ricky didn't know if he should hug or hit him. "Where . . . where were you?" he demanded, trying to catch his breath.

"When?"

"Why weren't you at the mailbox?" he asked, taking hold of the railing to steady himself, his rubbery legs beginning to cramp.

"Ma came home," said Matt.

Swiping at the sweat that had rolled into his eyes, Ricky looked toward the driveway, his vision slightly blurred by the salty sting. "But the . . ."

"It broke down. They had to tow it to Finks' Station." Matt took a few steps in Ricky's direction. "You okay?"

Ricky leaned back against the railing, then let himself sink to a sitting position. "My legs," he said, and, holding his breath, he began to massage first one, then the other.

Matt sat down across from him, Buddha-style. "That's only part of it," he said.

The knot in Ricky's left calf was as hard as a rock, and when he tried to flex his foot to relieve the cramp, it sent a shooting pain right up his leg and into his hip.

"We're gonna bury him the Saturday after Easter."

Ricky looked up from his kneading fingers and stared at his brother.

"We are," said Matt. "That's what Ma said. She was

on her way back from the funeral place when the car died."

About time, thought Ricky. He tried to read the expression on Matt's face. Happy? He couldn't tell.

"Been in her room crying since she got home."

Ricky suddenly had the urge to hit something. He dug his thumbs into the knotted muscle and kept the pressure on, the pain causing him to wince. Figures he'd have to go and die in the winter just to make their lives more miserable—Matt with his nightmares, and now his mother in there crying. " 'Cause of *him*?"

"Nah," said Matt. "Think about the car, 'cause she keeps saying, 'How am I supposed to get to work now?' I was trying to clean the house up for her so she'd feel better. Got our bed made up anyhow."

Ricky heard the wounded anger in his brother's voice but was too ashamed to look up. For weeks he'd tried everything he could think of to make Matt stop giving Bugsie lip on the bus. But Matt wouldn't listen to reason or Ricky's threats to beat him up, or his offers to pay him money. Then, last week, Lyle had given Ricky an update on the bus situation.

"Your brother's got balls the size of a bull's," he'd said. "Went and told Bugsie right to his face, 'You can take a flying leap into Loon Lake, asshole, 'cause I'm not scared of anyone with freckles on their wiener.' I figured it was curtains for sure, but the second after he said it, Slowpoke Clara tripped and fell getting off the bus, and 'cause she was wearing one of those short skirts of hers, all the guys raced for the windows to see if they could get a look at her underpants. That's the only thing that saved him. You got to do something, Ricky. If he don't stop, I'm gonna have an asthma attack for real."

And that was when Ricky had said he was going to tell all of Matt's friends he slept with a frying pan and wet the bed. Since the day he'd made that threat, this was the most they'd spoken. Even their mother had noticed the angry silence between them and had asked what the matter was, but neither would tell. It'd been hard letting Matt be mad at him, especially in the middle of the night after Matt wet their bed and sat there crying and glaring at him like he was a traitor. But the threat was the only way to keep Matt's mouth shut, and though Ricky hated himself for it, he hadn't given in. Until now.

"When you and Boomer weren't at the mailbox, I thought Wavin' Beady's murderer had got you or something." He ran his tongue over his chapped lips and swallowed hard, his parched throat feeling like sandpaper. "Made me feel bad about what I said about you giving Bugsie lip. I was just trying to . . ." Ricky didn't finish. He couldn't think of the right words to say.

"Stop me from sticking up for you?" Matt asked sarcastically, putting an end to the temporary truce. "I'm the one who has to ride the bus and listen to what they say about you. Ever think of that? Ever think how *I* feel—not being able to say a friggin' thing 'cause your spy's sitting there and you'll tell everyone I wet the . . ."

"I wouldn't do that."

"You said you would. You Scouts' Honored it." Matt got up and, giving him that traitor glare, added, "You're just like *him*."

"I am not!" yelled Ricky, watching his brother storm into the house.

"I'm not!" Ricky repeated, but as he sat there nursing his sore muscles and brooding, something Matt had said earlier came back to him. The Flying Monkeys were now a family joke, but when Ricky was little, he'd been petrified by those creatures from *The Wizard of Oz*, and his father had used that fear against him. *If you don't stop bawling, I'm gonna get the Flying Monkeys after you!* Ricky could still remember the terror he'd felt back then, how he'd scream and cry, truly believing that his father would send those horrible monkeys after him.

Flying Monkeys or wetting the bed—it was all the same. Ricky had done to Matt what his father had done to him. An icy feeling ran through him. He shivered and rubbed at the goose bumps prickling the hair on his arms.

· · ■ · ·

When Ricky went into the house, his mother's door was closed, and Katie was curled up on the living-room floor with her "stinky blanket" and "best pal,"

Boomer, whose belly she liked to use for a pillow. Boomer rolled his eyes up at Ricky but didn't move his body an inch, and wouldn't until Katie was done taking her nap. He should have known that's why Boomer hadn't been waiting for him—wherever Katie was, Boomer was. Out of all of them, she loved their dog the best, and their mother said it was because Boomer paid her the most attention.

He found his brother in the kitchen, standing on a chair and doing his best to wash the dishes. For a moment he just stood there staring at Matt's narrow shoulders, trying to swallow the knot of sorrow in his throat. He loved Matt so much that it'd always hurt less to take the blows when their father was on the warpath than to watch his little brother get it. When their father was alive they'd stuck to each other like glue. It was always them against *him*, and them against the world. Ricky wanted that back.

"Maybe I'm like him some," he confessed to Matt. He touched his brother's back softly. "But I don't say I'm sorry 'less I mean it."

Matt turned and looked at him, his blue eyes questioning that truth while his hand dripped soapsuds on the floor. "You mean I can say anything I want on the bus and you won't tell anybody?"

"That, too."

Matt studied him a moment longer, then nodded his head. "Guess we're brothers again then."

"Yeah," said Ricky, smiling with sudden joy. "So get

58

down from there. I'll do the dishes, you sweep and take out the trash."

For an hour or more, the two of them worked to clean the place up. Ricky finished the dishes and cleaned off the counter and table. Matt swept the floors and shook the rugs outside. Ricky wiped down the inside of the refrigerator and put the macaroni and cheese that had been in there since Sunday in Boomer's bowl. Matt picked up the newspapers in the living room and put away their backpacks and jackets and Katie's toys. Ricky scrubbed the hardened trail of toothpaste out of the bathroom sink. Matt folded the clean laundry and Ricky helped put it away. Both tiptoed by their mother's closed door every time they passed it, careful not to step on the place in the hallway that creaked.

When they were done cleaning, they started supper, talking in soft voices as they worked.

"Think we'll have to do that church thing again?" Matt asked.

"I don't think so, we already did that," said Ricky. "I think all we're going to do is go to the cemetery and bury him next to Grandma Gordon and his brother that died in the war."

"I'm tired of peeling," said Matt, kicking at the paper bag between his feet. "That enough for mash potatoes?"

Ricky, who was filling up a pot of water, looked over his shoulder at the pile. "Do two more. You know how

Ma is, she won't eat any unless there's enough for everyone."

"Yeah," Matt agreed. "Last night she wouldn't even have no chicken."

Ricky put the pot on the stove and turned the gas on. For a few seconds he watched the blue flame lick the burner. Once, when he was little, he had stood on a chair and was about to play with the knobs on the stove when his father caught him. He had turned on the burner and held Ricky's hand over it until the flame began to parch his skin and his screams brought his mother to the rescue. *We ain't got to worry 'bout him touching that stove again.* It was something Ricky thought of whenever he turned on the gas.

"Wonder if they'll let Uncle Bear and Uncle Carl come again," said Matt, adding his last potato to the pile.

"I hadn't even thought about that," said Ricky, remembering how the two uniformed guards had ushered his uncles into the funeral home before all the other people arrived for the wake. Ricky'd stood there like a statue, watching them cry: Uncle Bear, who was in prison for selling drugs and beating up a cop, and Uncle Carl, doing time for breaking into the summer homes on Loon Lake, possession of stolen goods, and something else. Although he'd always hated it when his father said, *You're gonna end up just like your uncles,* he'd felt embarrassed for them standing in that stupid room with its red carpet and flowers—Uncle Bear trying to kneel down in front of the closed casket and almost falling because of his chains; Uncle Carl trying to brush tears out of his real eye with cuffed hands. Although Ricky had been glad his father was lying in that casket where he couldn't hurt them anymore, he'd felt sorry for his uncles—if it'd been his brother, he'd have been crying, too.

"I hope they don't," Matt said firmly. "I didn't like them being there, crying and stuff. 'Sides, Uncle Carl scares me with that glass eye of his. Especially when he takes it out and soaks it in a cup. 'Member that time you and me had to sleep over their house 'cause the old man was too drunk to drive home and Uncle Bear wouldn't give him the keys?"

Ricky laughed. "Yeah. You got up in the middle of the night for a drink of water and started screaming your head off. I thought the old man was beating on you or something."

"You would have screamed your head off, too, if you'd looked in that cup and seen Uncle Carl's eye staring back at you."

Imitating his uncle's voice, Ricky said, "I only got twenty vision 'cause of your daddy. Coulda been a pilot like I wanted, if he hadn't poked me in the eye with that darn ski pole."

Matt started giggling. "That sounds just like him," he said; then his smile slowly disappeared. "I hope Aunt June the Loon don't come to the cemetery, neither. The way she kept howling in front of all those people—sounded worse than Boomer when we're pulling out porcupine quills. Thought Aunt Donna was gonna clobber her in the church."

"Well, we know Grampy Gordon won't be there," said Ricky, opening a can of beef stew. "He didn't even show up the last time. He was probably having his other leg cut off."

"Been so long since I've seen him, I can't 'member what he looks like."

Ricky searched his memory. "Uglier than Uncle Carl and crazier than Aunt June. Last time I saw him, I was about your age. It was at that Togus place. They'd cut his leg off 'cause it got infected or something. The old man made me go with him to visit. Grampy Gordon didn't even know who I was; kept calling me Willy; kept wanting me to look at his leg that wasn't there." Ricky shuddered. "Don't care if I ever see him again."

Matt was now sitting at the table drawing a picture, his crayons fanned out in front of him. "So you think it'll only be us then?" he asked.

Ricky tested the potatoes with a fork. "Probably," he said. "Saturday is Aunt Donna and Aunt Lane's busiest day at the Cut and Curl. Ma won't ask them to close the shop down 'cause of him." Ricky didn't bother to mention his grandparents on his mother's side. They lived in Florida now, but even when they'd lived in Harmony Center, he and Matt never got to see them—it was one of his father's rules.

Ricky replaced the cover and cranked the gas to

high. "Those spuds are hard as rocks," he told Matt. "Gonna be a while." He sat down at the table and watched Matt, whose head was bent over his drawing. Yesterday we wouldn't have been sitting in the same room together, he thought to himself. It was funny how "sorry" could change things if you meant it. To his father it'd been no more important than the word "hi" or "bye"—something a person said so often they didn't even think about it. Only time "sorry" meant something to him was when he'd say, *I'll* make *you* sorry. Ricky was relieved Matt was talking to him again. It meant a lot that his brother still believed him when he said he was sorry. "What are you drawing?"

Matt slid the picture around so Ricky could see it—a sun, grass, tombstones, and four stick figures wearing party hats.

· · ■ · ·

Ricky had just finished mashing the potatoes when they heard their mother's door open and then a creak in the hall.

"Here she comes," whispered Matt. "How's the table look?"

Matt had set the table with the good plates they only used on holidays—the ones their mother had bought at the Nelsons' "Wicked Big Garage Sale." He'd also put out real glasses instead of plastic cups, and had drawn pictures on each of the paper-towel napkins. "Looks just like a real restaurant," Ricky told him.

Their mother came into the kitchen, her eyes

red-rimmed, her hand running through her rumpled hair. "Where's Katie?"

"Still napping with Boomer," said Matt.

Looking down at the table, their mother asked, "What's all this?"

"Supper will be ready in a minute," Ricky told her. "I made your favorite: mash potatoes."

"I peeled them," said Matt, "and set the table, too." Matt pulled out the good chair that didn't have any loose legs. "Sit right here, Ma. Me and Ricky will take care of everything. He's the cook and I'm the waiter."

Their mother sat down and looked around the kitchen appreciatively. "Thank you for cleaning up, boys. You did a nice job."

"You'd better wake up Katie now," Ricky told Matt. "It'll be ready by the time you change her."

"I'm glad to see you two are talking to each other again," his mother said after Matt left the room. "At least something good's happened today. Did he tell you about the car?"

"It's a piece of junk, Ma," said Ricky. "You can see the road if you lift up the carpet." He ladled out a small portion of stew for Katie, then started to cut up the beef into tiny pieces so she wouldn't choke. He could hear her irritated grunts from the other room—their baby sister was always ugly when she got up from a nap.

"I didn't even know the inspection had run out," his mother sighed. "Mr. Finks showed me the sticker. It ran out three years ago; he said he'd be stealing from me if he put any work into it. God forgive me, but I wish your father had taken the car that night instead of the truck."

"Can you go to the bank and get a loan for another one?" asked Ricky.

"I wish it were that easy. We'll be lucky if they don't take the roof over our heads for all that I owe because of him."

Ricky looked up at the water stains on the ceiling, thinking, Who'd want it?

"I'm just thankful we didn't have to pay for his funeral. Mr. O'Malley still won't tell me who did. I asked again while I was there this afternoon; 'a friend of the family' is all he'll say." His mother shook her head and looked down at her hands. "Who in their right mind would be a friend of this family?"

Ricky looked at her sharply. "Lyle is," he said, defensively.

"Oh, I didn't mean you, sweetie, I meant your father and the rest of his crazy tribe. What I should have said was, Who in this town would pay for Willy Gordon's funeral? That casket alone must have cost a small fortune."

"Yeah," said Ricky. "Aunt Lane said whoever it was should have picked him out a pine box and bought us a dryer instead."

His mother chuckled. "Sounds just like her. If it'd been up to your Aunt Lane, she would have had him cremated and buried in a beer bottle. I'm not going to ask her or Aunt Donna to come. I don't want them closing down the shop on account of him. They've done enough for us already."

I was right, thought Ricky. "What about Uncle Carl and Uncle Bear?"

"I don't want to turn this into a circus, Ricky. . . ."

Guess Aunt June won't be coming either, he thought.

". . . I just want it over with so we can get on with our lives."

"Want a drink!" demanded Katie, marching into the kitchen with her blanket dragging behind her.

Ricky looked down at his little sister, who, like him, had the Gordon brown eyes and black hair. "What's the magic word?"

"Now?" she asked.

"Close enough." He lifted her up, and when she rested her head on his shoulder, Ricky caught the sour smell of Boomer in her silky hair. He carried her over to the table, and Matt helped him get her into the booster chair.

Pointing at the plates on the table, Katie looked up at Ricky with a wide-eyed stare. "Santa coming?"

...Chapter Six

In his dream, Ricky was back in that room with the blood-red carpet and sweet-smelling flowers. Katie was dancing in her new "pat pats" and Christmas dress, singing "Jingle Bells." It was his job to keep track of her and keep her quiet. "Shhh! Daddy's sleeping," he told her, but she wouldn't listen, kept twirling like a top on the toes of her shiny black patent-leather shoes. And then someone started pushing at him from behind, and he felt like he was walking through lake water as he drew closer and closer to the wooden box. His legs were heavy and it hurt to lift them, but all the faces were watching and waiting—*Hurry up and take your turn,* they were saying, though none had mouths. Then, suddenly, he noticed the symmetrical pattern tooled into the chestnut-colored wood, a one-inch border of semicircles flowing in one continuous line, each arc rising and falling exactly the same. It was beautiful, but when he reached out to trace it, a hand grabbed his wrist. It was his father, somehow alive again and staring right at him, *You're going to get it!* burning in his eyes.

Ricky woke with a start and began to battle with the blanket that was tangled around him. He flailed his arms, trying to free himself from its grip and the nightmare that still held him. Believing his father was after him, he bolted off the couch and started to run. He made it all the way to the front door before he finally realized he was awake. It was morning. His heart drumming in his chest, his body shaking, Ricky turned and scanned the room—no one was there but him.

．．■．．

Ten minutes later he was running down the middle of the road, the soft slap of his shoes against the pavement keeping time with the chant inside his head—*Go...go...go...*

The overcast sky was dull gray, the air heavy with moisture. Fog lifted like smoke off Mr. Lewis' garden. It was earlier than usual so Ricky had the road to himself; he didn't have to keep to the shoulder, where the sand would suck at his shoes and new blisters. There was no one else to worry about—just himself and that imaginary line he ran along. From point A, home, to point B, school, he knew every bend, hill, and pothole. The road had become as familiar as that secret tree in the woods—an old beech that never lost dead leaves in winter, whose smooth gray limbs had kept him safe when he was little and needed a place to escape to.

This morning he wanted to escape from point A and that dream as fast as he could. He was running with an urgency he couldn't control, the chant in his head driving his arms and legs as he sprinted down the road through the quiet and fog. *Go . . . go . . . go . . .* spurred him on past the woods and the sad, haunting call of a mourning dove; *go . . . go . . . go . . .* pushed him past the misty bog with its weeping willows and pools of muddy water; *go . . . go . . . go . . .* sent him down that imaginary line in the center of the road until his chest felt like someone was standing on it.

By the time he passed the Bensons', his legs had turned to butter and the chant had been replaced by a ringing in his head. He staggered to the side of the road, and his knees buckled beneath him. Leaning forward, he braced himself with his arms, his fingers splayed against the sand, and retched like a dog. The muscles in his stomach contracted violently, but each heave brought forth only salty spit after that initial stream of yellow water.

When the nausea began to subside, he opened his eyes. A long string of drool was hanging from his lip, and he brushed it away with his sandy fingers. He glanced around, thankful that it was morning and there hadn't been anyone around to see him puke. He crawled a few feet away, then sat and waited for his quivering body to recover. This was the first time he'd gotten sick and it scared him. What had gone wrong?

He rubbed his hands against his pant legs, then pulled a notebook out of his backpack. From the day after Slowpoke Clara had caught him scratching those equations in the sand, he'd been faithfully recording his times each morning and afternoon. Because he didn't own a watch that worked, he'd used the clock on the kitchen stove and the one in his classroom to go by. He'd made graphs of those numbers to keep track of his progress. He also charted his weekly average speed against the distance of 3.5 miles, allowing him to project how fast he should be going by a certain date. And every day he'd noted any other data he felt might have had an effect on time for that entry: "raining"; "bad blister on right foot"; "up with Matt again last night"; "breathe in through nose, out through mouth = less cramps."

He flipped through the dog-eared pages of "Jogging" until he came to the new section he'd begun just last week: "Running." His pencil slid along some of the observations. "Harder to run than jog." "Made it to Lyle's." "Running = new blisters." "Up with Matt." "Bus passed me at lightning tree."

Then he wrote down the date, and under A.M. scribbled: "too fast = puke."

It was a mistake he wouldn't make again.

.. ■ ..

That Friday had started off bad and went downhill from there. His teacher Mrs. Parker was sick, and her substitute, as Lyle said, was older than Hatchet Mountain and just as big. They'd had her before, and

Ricky knew it wasn't going to be an easy day—her nickname in his school was "Go to the Office." It was practically the only thing she said. Once she'd sent Wen Webber down to Mr. Daniels just for sneezing too loud. The only time she didn't say "Go to the office" was when a kid asked to go to the bathroom; then it was "You'll have to wait until recess."

As soon as she walked through the door, Lyle leaned over and whispered, "We might as well go down to the office right now and get it over with."

Yeah, thought Ricky, first I puked, and now Go to the Office—I never should have gotten off the couch.

He looked out the window and his spirits took an even deeper dive. The gray sky had finally given in—it was raining. He wondered briefly if his mother and Katie had made it up to Mrs. Chaffee's yet or if they were still on their way, his mother pushing Katie's carriage through the rain. Although it made him feel bad for them, his main concern about the weather was that it meant indoor recess, which, with the "Wait until recess" lady here, meant he'd have to hold it all day.

Since he'd made his deal with Mr. Daniels, Ricky had never used the bathroom during recess until all the kids were outside on the playground, and on those days it had rained, Mrs. Parker, who knew his situation with Bugsie, had always allowed him to go during class, when the odds of running into Bugsie were small. He looked away from the window and narrowed his eyes at the woman he now held responsible for the suffering he'd have to face. Just the sound of the rain, and the idea of not being allowed to go, made him want to take a leak.

Go to the Office was at the blackboard now, writing down the assignments they were supposed to do while she ate doughnuts and did crossword puzzles. Knowing she couldn't see him, Lyle was pantomiming, shoving imaginary doughnuts into his mouth in rapid succession, first with one hand and then the other. Everyone around him, including Ricky, cracked up.

At the sound of their stifled laughter, the substitute turned her head just enough to glare over her shoulder. "Is something funny?"

No one moved, or answered the question.

"Then get busy," she ordered.

In an instant, the room was filled with bent heads over pens and pencils. The first assignment, as usual, was Journal Entry. Every day since school started, Mrs. Parker had made them write a paragraph or more each day in the thin baby-blue books they used for journals. They could write anything they wanted, and although the blue books were read and corrected for spelling, they were never graded. Ricky was glad they weren't, for he knew that if they were, his D in English would be an F instead. He hated writing.

He looked over at Lyle, whose pencil was already flying across a new page in his blue book. Lyle always had something to write. He was a walking encyclopedia when it came to cows. It amazed Ricky that Lyle had trouble doing his math homework but could look at a cow and know how much it weighed and how much milk it would give, and could rattle off facts and numbers about breeding them without even thinking. It was a language of numbers Ricky had never come across in any of his math books—one he didn't even understand, though they stuck in his head.

He looked down at the blue lines on the blank page in front of him. Usually he couldn't think of anything to write until the twenty minutes were almost over, so he'd gotten in the habit of writing big to make it look like he'd done more than he had. He glanced over at Slowpoke Clara, who probably wrote faster than Stephen King. Clara hadn't gotten her nickname because of her schoolwork—she'd already gone through about ten of those stupid blue books, while he was still struggling to get through his second, big writing and all. She was Slowpoke because she always took her time, like the rest of the world was just there to wait for her. He figured if her house was on fire she'd probably get dressed, brush out her hair, and make her bed before she bothered to walk out her bedroom door. He tried to look away from her, but his eyes couldn't stop staring at the silky blond hair clinging to her pale-yellow sweater. It made him envy Tom and wonder what they did while their bikes were hidden in the bushes. Maybe she was writing about it in her blue book right now.

Just then, Clara's pen stopped moving. She turned and caught his stare, the small smile on her pouty lips making him think for a terrifying moment that she'd been reading his mind. He quickly looked down at his blue book, his face hot and itchy. Write something, he told himself, but three minutes later, when the journals were collected by the first person in each row, he still hadn't written even one big word. It was only after he'd passed in his blue book that he thought of something he could have written about. The day before, during library time, he'd found a book on running. He could have written about that Greek guy named Pheidippides, who'd run all the way to Athens to let the people know their troops had won the battle in Marathon. He could have told how the poor guy'd run twenty-six miles and 385 yards to get there, and how, right after he told them they'd won, he'd keeled over and died from exhaustion. It would have been a good thing to write about, and as Ricky watched Tammy carry the pile of blue books up to the teacher's desk, he began to wonder how old Pheidippides was, how long it had taken him, and if he'd had to stop and puke a couple of times along the way. He couldn't imagine running twenty-six miles—he'd barely made it past the Bensons' this morning.

The next assignment on the list was a spelling test.

"Clear your desks," ordered the substitute as she passed out the lined yellow paper. "And keep your eyes on your own work and not your neighbors'," she warned.

Ricky glanced at the clock—five of nine. They'd be at the Chaffees' by now—Katie playing with the little kids and his mother probably already at the sewing machine. Cindy Chaffee used to be a tailor in a fancy women's shop over in Camden, and had made wedding dresses on the side. She quit her job when her first baby was born, and from then on made kids' clothes instead of wedding dresses. Her handmade outfits sold so fast in the tourist shops on the coast that she now had two women besides his mother working for her.

Cindy and his mother had been friends since they were little. His father had had rules about her, too, like he had about Ricky's aunts, but that had never stopped Cindy from coming over to their house, or calling Ricky's mother up on the phone—she just did it when *he* wasn't around. His father called Cindy "That Troublemaker" and was always blaming her for putting ideas in Ricky's mother's head. *You'll go to work for her over my dead body.* And that's just what his mother had done. Now she worked five days a week making kids' clothes that only rich people could afford.

"Word number one," said the substitute, then looked up from the paper she was holding. "Imagination."

Ricky pulled himself away from thoughts of his mother and wrote down the word.

"Word number two. Accomplishment."

The class was waiting for word number three when Lyle broke wind, a little squeaker loud enough to make everyone giggle into their hands. Everyone except for Lyle and the teacher, who was glaring at him like he'd just committed murder.

"I didn't mean to," he tried to explain to her. "I had bacon for breakfast."

Another round of giggles, and Go to the Office lived up to her name.

Ricky watched Lyle shuffle down the aisle, hands deep in his pockets, eyes on the floor. When he got to the door, Lyle turned and raised his arms like a boxer who'd just won a fight. All the kids snickered. The teacher snapped her head around to see what the students were staring at, but by then the victor had already danced out the door.

Trying to restore order, or maybe save face, she said, "Word number three."

·· ■ ··

The hard April rain knocked at the windows and blurred the glass. In a corner of the classroom, the fish tank bubbled while Mr. Blue Fish and Beta darted in and out of their colorful castle. All that water, thought Ricky, and no way to have a drink. The inside of his mouth felt like toast. It made him regret that he'd only taken a few sips from the water fountain when he'd gotten to school. But a lesson he'd learned early on had stopped him: too much water after jogging = stomachache.

He looked away from the fish tank. Slowpoke Clara was curling her hair with her fingers; Jeff Walker was digging in his nose with one of his; Tina was staring out the window and probably thinking about her horses. Like them, Ricky was bored with silent reading.

If Mrs. Parker were there, it would have been over fifteen minutes ago and they'd be halfway through science, the only other subject he liked besides math.

Ricky's stomach gurgled—he hadn't eaten since supper the night before. He looked down at the new time graph he'd been charting in his notebook while he was supposed to be reading. He could no longer concentrate on the numbers, his head was so floaty; just a minute ago, he couldn't even remember the simple formula $r = d \div t$.

He looked up at the clock. Thirteen point five more minutes until recess. Eight hundred and ten seconds till they could get up and stretch, go to the bathroom, eat snacks. Just the thought of eating the Cheerios in his bread bag caused his stomach to rumble painfully. And it was then that he remembered how he'd left in such a hurry. He hadn't even bothered to wash his face or comb his hair, and he'd forgotten in his haste to refill the bread bag in his backpack. Automatically he glanced at Lyle, whose stay with Mr. Daniels had been just long enough for him to admit that he'd farted by mistake. I wonder what he brought, thought Ricky, knowing Lyle would share with him. Crackers? His mother's chocolate-chip cookies? Fruit Roll-Ups? The suspense was killing him.

At 320 seconds, his stomach growled so loudly that he glanced up front, certain that Go to the Office would send him down for disturbing the peace. But the teacher still had her nose in her crossword book, which was thicker than a dictionary. He turned to Lyle, who had a book propped up with one hand to look like he was reading while he drew a cow's udder with the other. Ricky couldn't wait another second. "What'd you bring for snack?" he whispered.

Lyle gave him a look that said, *Are you crazy?*, but after checking on the enemy, he lowered his head so his face was hidden behind his book and mouthed back, "Devil Dog." And then Lyle did something that made Ricky thank Jesus—he held up two fingers.

By the time the bell finally rang five minutes later, Ricky could hardly wait to rip open that cellophane cover with his teeth. But then Go to the Office made an announcement that made his hunger disappear. "Make a line," she ordered. "And keep your lips locked in the hall on the way to the bathroom."

Ricky watched the kids line up, but he stayed in his seat.

"Hurry up, young man," said the teacher, looking back at him.

"I don't have to go," Ricky told her.

"I don't care if you do or not," she said. "Get in line."

"What he means is that he don't *have* to," Lyle tried to explain.

Pointing a stout finger at Lyle like a gun, she said, "Not another word out of you."

"But, he's got a deal with Mr. Daniels, and . . ."

The teacher latched on to Lyle's arm before he had a chance to finish. "I think you know the way to the office by now," she said, pushing him toward the door.

"I'm going, I'm going," Lyle told her, shaking off her

hold. "Jesum-crow," he continued under his breath, but loud enough for everyone to hear. "Hope he lets me stay there this time."

As she watched him go, the teacher mumbled under her breath, too. "Biggest mistake they ever made was taking the stick out of a teacher's hand." Then she wheeled around and pinned Ricky with her beady eyes. "Do you want to join him?"

The truth was, he did. He wanted to be as far away from that woman with her white mustache and angry eyes as he could get. If Mr. Daniels' warning hadn't flashed into his mind at that very moment, he would have told that teacher to suck eggs and die.

But there was no way he'd let his mother walk from Cindy's to here in the pouring rain because of that witch, so he shook his head no, then got up and went to the end of the line.

"Looks could kill, she'd be dead," Jeff Walker whispered to him, as the line marched toward the bathrooms. "Thought you were gonna tell her where to go, for sure."

"Day ain't over yet," Ricky reminded him. Then he spotted Matt, who was on his way out of the boys' room. "Coast is clear," mouthed Matt on his way by, which meant Bugsie wasn't in there.

I might as well go while I have the chance, thought Ricky, and he followed Jeff and the others through the door.

He was zipping up when he heard Bugsie's voice, a cut above his friends', as the sixth-graders came in. For over a month Ricky had gone out of his way to avoid him. He'd even managed to ignore those remarks Bugsie made when there were too many teachers around for him to try something besides shooting his mouth off just loud enough for Ricky to hear. *Buck, buck, buck, there goes the Gordon Chicken. . . . Hey, Gordon, heard Colonel Sanders is looking for you. . . . Better take up boxin' instead of joggin', Gordon, 'cause one of these days I'm gonna get you alone.* It was this last threat that raced through Ricky's mind the second he heard Bugsie's voice.

Ricky turned around just in time to see the boys in his own class dash for the door like the place was on fire. Melonhead, who'd just been peeing beside him, didn't even stop long enough to close his fly.

Norman Calvert and Dan Simmons elbowed their way through the deserting crowd and stood behind their leader, who sniffed at the air and wrinkled his nose. "Smells like chickenshit to me," Bugsie told them. "Must be a Gordon around."

Ricky tried to walk by them, but Bugsie stepped in front of him. Norman and Dan crowded in; the three of them blocked the only exit. Ricky looked behind him— not even a window. He was trapped. Cornered like that time in the living room. The mop handle coming down on him over and over, its wood hard as metal. The whack and crack of flesh and bone; the searing pain between blows. The blood in his mouth dripping on the floor. He couldn't defend himself that day, but it was going to be a different story in this bathroom with its green walls that stank of urine. Stay cool, he told himself. Too fast = puke.

"Decisions, decisions," said Bugsie, placing a finger on his freckled chin. "Do I dunk your head in the toilet or beat your face in?"

Though there were three of them, Ricky kept his eyes on Bugsie. If he could hurt the leader, the pals would back off. But Bugsie was a lot bigger and had a longer reach. Even the odds, thought Ricky, and he began to look for weak points.

"Check the stalls, Norman," Bugsie ordered. "See if anyone forgot to flush."

Then Ricky saw it—Bugsie's baggy jeans. They were riding so low on his hips the top of his Hanes was showing. I know his plan, thought Ricky, but he don't know mine.

"Gross!" said Norman, as he came to the last stall before the urinals. "Here's one. Kid must've been workin' on that dump for a week."

Yank his pants down, thought Ricky, knock him over with a head butt, then kick him. He won't expect that, he'll expect a punch.

"Guess it's your lucky day, Gordon," said Bugsie, looking toward the stall.

Just as Ricky was about to make his move, Mr. Daniels barged through the door as though he were expecting trouble.

Guess it *is* my lucky day, thought Ricky.

"Something going on here?" asked Mr. Daniels.

Bugsie hesitated just long enough to get over his

surprise. "Just using the bathroom, Mr. Daniels," he said, feigning innocence. "Right, guys?"

Dan and Norman gave a guilty nod.

"You okay, Ricky?" asked Mr. Daniels. "These boys giving you any trouble?"

"We didn't touch him," said Bugsie.

"That's the truth, Mr. Daniels," added Norman, who was already on probation for getting caught in school with cigarettes. "Right, Ricky?" he pleaded, inching away from the stall.

It was a chance for Ricky to tell the principal what Bugsie's plan was, but Ricky didn't take it. In his mind the only thing worse than a chickenshit was a rat. "Yeah, that's right," said Ricky. "I was just going back to my room."

Norman let out a sigh of relief, and Dan Simmons, whose older brother was serving time in Windham, gave Ricky a slight nod of approval.

Bugsie, who figured Ricky was too scared of him to tell the truth, smiled and said, "Toldja."

"In that case, you boys get back to your rooms, too," the principal ordered. "I have enough students spending time in my office this morning for nothing."

· · ■ · ·

When Ricky got to his classroom, Lyle was back from exile and Go to the Office was the one who was missing.

"You'll never believe what happened," Ricky told him, sliding into his seat.

82

"Let me guess," said Lyle, pushing his glasses up over his nose. "You're here, and you ain't bleeding; Mr. Daniels must have gotten there in time. Never seen him run like that. Come to think of it, that's the first time I've ever seen him run."

"*You* told him?" asked Ricky.

"Saw Bugsie and his boys headed down there on my way to the office. Just figured I better tell someone." Lyle handed him a Devil Dog. "Saved this one for you."

"Thanks," said Ricky, taking it from him. "And for telling Daniels, too. I'd probably be on my way home if you didn't."

"Or on your way to the hospital," Lyle pointed out.

Ricky glanced over at Melonhead and Jeff Walker, who were eating their snacks and playing hangman. "Good to know I've got one friend in this friggin' school. You should have seen them split on me. Speaking of enemies, where'd she go?" he asked, nodding toward the front of the room. "Run out of doughnuts or something?"

"Soon as Garvey stopped by to tell her he'd be in to teach math, she was out the door. Probably down the teachers' lounge complaining about me and stocking up on jelly rolls. But forget about her, give me the details before Chalky gets here."

"Chalky" was the kids' nickname for Mr. Garvey, who tended to get so excited when he was teaching that he'd use his arm instead of an eraser to wipe the blackboard clean. He also had a habit of running his hand through his hair when he was thinking of a way to explain things, so his hair was usually chalky, too. But Ricky never used the nickname for his favorite teacher; he had too much respect for him.

"Later," Ricky now told Lyle. "Here comes Mr. Garvey."

･･■･･

The incident in the bathroom had shaken Ricky up. It was too close a call—if Mr. Daniels had waited another ten seconds, he would have caught Ricky yanking Bugsie's pants down. Then where would he be? Suspended for sure; his deal with Daniels and his promise to his mother, history. Bugsie would have denied he'd ever had a plan, and walked out of the bathroom smelling like a rose. No matter how many times Ricky weighed the possibilities, he kept coming up with the same answer. Even if he'd managed to knock Bugsie on his butt and get a few kicks in before Mr. Daniels had come flying through that door, he still would have been the loser.

"What's the matter with you, Ricky?" Mr. Garvey asked. The two of them were working one-on-one in the corner while the rest of the class took a test. "You don't need to write that out, do it in your head; you know this stuff backward."

Embarrassed, Ricky stared down at his paper. He couldn't concentrate—his mind kept wandering back to that bathroom. "Sorry," Ricky told him, and he was.

To him Mr. Garvey was God—he understood numbers and went out of his way to teach Ricky. "I can't think today."

"This isn't like you," said Mr. Garvey, running his fingers and new streaks of white through his dark hair. "Is something the matter? Are you feeling sick?"

He was sick all right: sick of dealing with Bugsie, sick of school, sick of home and all the worry that went with it. Sick of being a Gordon. "I'm just tired," he told him.

"I think maybe I've been pushing you too hard, Ricky. You're so capable and hungry for it, I sometimes forget how young you are. So we're going to forget about this chapter today, and do something different while they're taking their test. We'll play."

"Play?" asked Ricky.

"That's right. Play." Mr. Garvey stuck his hand in his pocket and pulled out some change. "Don't look," he said, covering up his hand. "Okay, I have forty-six cents, four coins in all, two are the same. What are the coins?"

"A penny, two dimes, and a quarter," said Ricky, then started laughing. "Too easy."

Mr. Garvey smiled. "Sixty-three dollars in change, six hundred coins in all: what are they?"

"Three hundred pennies, one hundred dimes, two hundred quarters," Ricky answered. "I like this game."

"And that's my point, Ricky. Sometimes you have to stop and let yourself play or you might forget why it's fun. Don't burn yourself out, son. You're already two years ahead of the others."

·· ■ ··

Besides Lyle, Go to the Office sent three other students down to Mr. Daniels for trivial offenses that day. But Ricky wasn't one of them. He behaved so well that, by the time the afternoon bell finally rang, he was exhausted.

"I got to get out of here," he told Lyle as they went to grab their jackets. "Being good's killing me."

A minute later, while students were lining up by the office and boo-hooing about getting wet between the building and the waiting buses, Ricky bolted through the school's front door and out into the driving rain.

He followed the sidewalk past the three yellow buses. "Better ride today, Ricky!" Mr. Mack called to him. But Ricky waved him off and kept on going.

The playground was swollen with puddles, and where it wasn't, the grass was spongy and slick beneath the smooth soles of his shoes. He slipped and almost fell more than once before he reached the woods. Although the swaying branches above him gave some shelter from the rain, it was harder going, the dirt path like quicksand, the mud so thick he ran right out of one shoe. Hopping back to get it, he stumbled, and the next thing he knew he was face down in the mud. He sat up and checked the damage—hands, arms, legs, feet; everything could move without hurting. Then he looked down at the layer of mud smeared on his jacket, jeans, and the shoeless foot whose white sock was now brown. I give up, he thought. All the day's frustration had finally caught up with him, and because there was no one there to see him, he let himself cry.

What am I trying to prove anyhow? he wondered, looking back at his shoe that was still angled in the mud. Who cares if I ever beat the bus? For a minute or more, he just sat there listening to the pines whispering in the windswept rain, crying and staring at his shoe as though it could give him an answer or a reason to get up. Only one who cares, he finally told himself, is me.

He walked the rest of the way out of the woods, blazing his own trail to avoid the muddy path and another risky fall. Though he knew the race was over for the day, when he reached the asphalt on Route 26 he started running again.

Narrowing his eyes against the wind and rain, he tried to find his rhythm, but his gait was awkward: his arms and legs were out of sync. His soaked clothing and mud-caked shoes were dragging him down, making him feel like he was running in place.

He turned onto Ridge Road, the hammering rain now slanting at him from the side, stinging his right ear and cheek. Inside his socks, he could feel water and grit squishing between his toes. When he ran past the Williamses', the dog that was always waiting for him was nowhere to be seen.

He'd only gone down Ridge Road a short distance when the toilet paper inside his shoes started to bother him. Waterlogged and lumpy, it was chafing at his blisters, causing a burning pain to shoot up the back of his legs. After limping to the side of the road, he took off his shoes, scooped out the soggy paper, and threw the rocklike wads into the bushes. Then he peeled back the wet sock on the heel that hurt the worst and cringed in pain. The skin all around the blister had parboiled. All that was left of the dime-sized scab was a yellowish ooze with a hole in the center that exposed the red, raw surface beneath. The blister on the other heel was a new one and hadn't yet broken. With a tender finger, he probed at the bubble of water beneath the skin.

The thought of pulling his wet socks and shoes back on depressed him. He'd rather go barefoot, he decided. He shoved his socks in the toes of his shoes, then knotted two laces together. After slinging the shoes over his left shoulder, he headed straight for the deepest puddle and waded in. The frigid water numbed the burning blisters as he stood there swirling his feet. He could feel the mud that had collected between his toes loosening and he started to wiggle them against the puddle's sandy bottom, the color of his skin through the muddying water reminding him of the underbellies of Loon Lake fish. He lifted one foot just enough to break the surface with his wiggling toes. "They're really biting today, Matt," he said, smiling. "Always hungry when it's raining."

He cuffed up the muddy ends of his jeans, then splashed his way out of the puddle, his feet so happy they started running. Without his shoes on, Ricky felt so free that he no longer noticed the rain. His feet tingled each time his bare soles touched the cold surface of the road. How easy it was to lift his feet! His arms and legs had found the rhythm without his even trying. It was like his naked feet had magically sprouted wings and he could suddenly fly effortlessly past the Bakers' farm pond and Slowpoke Clara's, the energy soaring inside him feeling better than Christmas. He was running free and easy with a smile on his face, running down Ridge Road through puddles and rain just because it felt so good.

Chapter Seven

On the day they were to bury his father, Ricky woke up so early the windows in the living room were still black. Staring at the thin ray of light leaking in from the kitchen, he wondered what time it was and why the light was on. Too tired to lift his head off the pillow, he shut his eyes and listened as the house spoke to him—the creak and groan of the ironing board, the hissing of steam, the peaceful sound of his mother humming "Amazing Grace." "You up, Ma?" he asked.

"Go back to sleep, Ricky," she called softly. "You don't have to be up for a couple of hours yet."

Pulling the blanket around him more tightly, he asked, "Want me to feed the fire?"

"It's okay," she told him. "I already did. Now, get some sleep, sweetie; we have a long day ahead of us."

Ricky rolled over and snuggled his face into the pillow, but he was now wide awake. The sleepy cobwebs in his mind had been swept away as soon as his mother had mentioned the long day to come. Today they were finally going to bury his father in Pine Grove Cemetery. It was the same place where Mrs. Lewis was buried. She had a rose-colored granite stone with a pretty etching of a chickadee sitting on a pine cone. The chickadee was Mrs. Lewis' favorite bird. She liked to say God created them so the people in Maine would have something to smile about during the winter.

Mrs. Lewis had died suddenly, too. One day Ricky was making cookies with her, and two days later she was dead. He'd learned of her death down at the general store. The words "Have you heard about Mathilda Lewis?" had slapped him in the face as soon as he'd followed his father through the door, the cow bell still announcing their entrance. The regulars, men who mostly worked in the mill or in the woods logging, or, in Roy Benson's case, running a dairy farm, were sitting on the bench in front of the woodstove as usual. Their weather talk was suspended just long enough for Diana, behind the counter, to finish saying, "Word is, she passed away on the operating table while the doctors were fixing her broken hip."

"Goddamn shame," his father had said, like he really cared, and all the men on the bench had nodded their heads at the same time, as though they were connected to the same invisible string.

Ricky had stood there, his mind unable to understand the true meaning of Diana's words. The *passed away* didn't begin to make sense until he read the grave expressions on those bobbing, tired faces whose eyes were staring down at rough hands, work boots, the worn, sagging floor. Even then he wasn't sure if dead and *passed away* were one and the same thing till he heard the word *was*. Mr. Chaffee's usually booming voice was a raspy whisper. "She was a great lady. Always doing for somebody."

That's how Ricky had found out that the old woman whom he'd come to love and trust like one of her leery jays—the one whose hands he'd let touch and feed him—had died. The somebody she was always doing for had stood there trying to swallow that *was* like a Loon Lake fish caught on a four-prong lure while everything around him went on as usual. The men bobbed their heads in the same exact way; Diana made Italian sandwiches behind the counter. The air filled his nostrils with smells of pizza, cigarette smoke, and chain-saw oil. His father moved toward the beer cooler without a backward glance or worry.

It had rained the day they'd buried Mrs. Lewis. Ricky had dressed up that morning in the best clothes he owned, then slid out his bedroom window, fearing his mother might try to stop him otherwise. He'd hidden in the woods behind the cemetery for what seemed like hours before the long black limousine and army of cars started coming up the winding road with their lights and windshield wipers on. Our Cop's Chevy, with its blue light flashing on the dashboard, led the way. Ricky was careful not to let them see him, since he wasn't supposed to be there. "Funerals are no place for children," his mother had told him,

" 'specially when they're not related." So he'd stayed hunkered down in the sumac, still as a stone, watching her casket being slowly carried to a hole in the earth that had been covered with a blanket of too-green plastic grass. He'd watched as the people began to get out of their vehicles, their umbrellas blooming like a garden of black flowers.

Even from a distance, he'd been able to recognize almost everybody. The Hendrickses, the Marshalls, the Bensons, and the Warren sisters, two old maids who always came to Mrs. Lewis' for tea and cribbage on Tuesdays. All the men from the mill and women from church. Old people with canes and white heads. Even Duckmaker was there, the town's war hero turned drunk, whom Mrs. Lewis had persuaded her husband to keep rehiring because he'd done his duty for his country. All of them were gathered among the graves in the gray rain to say prayers. Their voices reached him like a faint murmur, making him realize for the first time just how many people she'd "done for" besides him.

Ricky had wanted to be down there with them, placing one of those yellow roses on her casket like everyone else. He wanted to be with Mr. Lewis, who kept looking his way as though he knew Ricky was up there hiding in the sumac. Mr. Lewis, whom he feared and respected, whom he'd competed with for her affection, was looking older than the trees. He seemed like a lost kid, holding on to Mr. Chaffee's big arm—staring right at Ricky as though the sumac wasn't even there.

•• ■ ••

"Wake up," said Matt, shaking Ricky's shoulder. "We're having bacon!"

Ricky opened his eyes. The room was now full of sunlight. He must have dozed off.

"Eggs, too," said Matt, jumping up and down. "Scrambled."

Ricky stretched and rubbed his eyes. "I'll be there in a minute," he told Matt. "I just need to wake up."

"Snooze you lose," Matt warned him, then dashed off toward the kitchen.

Ricky could smell the rare and delicious scent of bacon floating in the air, and it made his mouth water. Still, he lay there a moment longer staring at the sunlight filtering through the plastic. He'd just assumed it would rain for his father's burial like it had for Mrs. Lewis', and like it did in all the movies. It made him wonder if the sky only cried if the dead person was worth it.

"Come on, Ricky," his mother called. "Breakfast is ready; time to get up."

"I'm coming," he told her, then rolled off the couch.

Katie was already in her booster chair chewing, a handful of eggs in one fist, a piece of jellied toast in the other. Ricky leaned over and gave the top of her head a kiss. Boomer was staring up at him from beneath the table, panting and waiting for Katie's small, sticky hands to give him a treat.

"Smells great, Ma," said Ricky, sliding into a chair.

"Well, eat it while it's still hot," said his mother, leaning over his shoulder to pour orange juice. "Then we have to get going. You boys need to take your showers and get dressed. We have to meet Father Bob at the cemetery by ten, and it will take us a little while to walk up there."

"Don't see why Aunt Donna can't give us a ride," said Matt, shoveling down his eggs.

"Because I didn't ask her to, that's why," said their mother. "Saturday is their busiest day at the shop. I'm not going to take money out of her pocket just to give us a ride across town when we can walk. Katie Marie, stop wasting your breakfast on that dog. I see your hands under the table."

Katie drew her hands back as though she'd touched something hot, then rolled her eyes in a way that made them all laugh.

"Look at you," their mother told her. "You have more eggs in your hair than in your stomach."

"Put her on the floor," said Matt. "Boomer will clean her up."

"Very funny," said their mother, lifting Katie out of her booster seat. "Come on, sweet pea. Time for a bath and shampoo; then you can put on your party dress."

Katie's face lit up. "Pat pats?" she asked.

"Yes, you can wear your pat-pat shoes, too," said their mother, carrying their little sister off toward the bathroom.

"Kinda feels like Easter again," said Matt, who'd already eaten six slices of bacon and was now eyeing the last piece on the plate. "Only thing missing's the jelly beans and new socks in our shoes."

Ricky turned his head and looked at their Sunday clothes, all pressed and arranged on hangers whose handles were straddling the open pantry door. Then he lowered his gaze to the mudless shoes lined up beneath; his worn-out pair shining with the gloss of Vaseline. It was a long enough look for his little brother to scarf up the last piece of bacon. "Hey," said Ricky when he turned back around and saw the plate was empty. "I only had two pieces!"

"Snooze you lose," said Matt again.

It was one of their father's sayings, and as Ricky looked back down at the empty plate he repeated another: "Early bird gets the worm."

"You're uglier than sin on Sunday," said Matt, catching on.

"I'll knock you into next Tuesday."

"Don't give me any lip, buster, or you'll be wearing this belt on your back."

"You're so full of crap, it's coming out of your ears," said Ricky, laughing.

"Yeah," said Matt, giving him a sad smile, "that was one of his favorites."

·· ■ ··

An hour later, Matt and Ricky sat on the couch, showered, dressed, and anxious to get moving.

"What's taking her?" asked Matt, yanking at the collar on his shirt. "This thing's strangling me."

Ricky felt as restless as his brother and wished he was out running. If it were a regular Saturday, he'd be at the mill working by now. He would have already had breakfast with Mr. Lewis, who liked to have venison with his runny eggs. Mr. Lewis made good biscuits and knew how to cook without burning things. He'd told Ricky he'd grown up without a mother so he'd had to learn. Ricky had gone over there the other night after supper to let him know he wouldn't be able to work this Saturday. He'd found Mr. Lewis sitting in the rocker on the front porch, smoking his pipe as evening came on. The sky was the color of a bruise, blue and purple with traces of black.

Although he'd once overheard Mrs. Lewis telling the Warren sisters, "Ricky's the son I was never blessed with," he'd always had the feeling that her husband thought of him as the son he never would have wanted. Ricky figured that to Mr. Lewis he was just that thieving kid down the road who'd stolen first rhubarb out of his garden, then Mrs. Lewis' love. In the beginning that wasn't something Ricky could have put into words, but even at a young age, he'd instinctively known Mr. Lewis didn't want him around when he was home. He could tell from the look on the old man's face when Mrs. Lewis would fill Ricky's glass first, and by the way he'd sulk and rattle his newspaper and keep checking his watch if he was home while they were making cookies or playing cards. After Mrs. Lewis died, Ricky didn't go over to their house for a long time, assuming that there was no longer any reason to and that Mr. Lewis wouldn't want him there anyway. It wasn't until Mr. Lewis saw him in the store one day and told him the grass needed mowing that he'd started going there again. "The job's still yours if you want it," Mr. Lewis had said gruffly. "Come by tomorrow afternoon at four o'clock, and don't be late."

At first it had felt strange being in their house without Mrs. Lewis there. He'd expected to smell cookies baking in the oven every time he walked into the kitchen. And sometimes, while he was weeding or pulling off potato bugs in the vegetable garden, he'd look up, thinking he'd see her in her straw hat and brown work gloves. But the quiet was the hardest thing for him to get used to—the absence of her limping shuffle across the linoleum floor; the silence of the radio that had played the classical stuff she liked, which never had words. He missed the sound of her voice telling stories in that matter-of-fact way, and her hiccuping laughter. He even missed the crisp sternness of her words when she was worked up about the government or the price of something or Mr. Lewis' not putting things back where they belonged.

It was also strange being there with just Mr. Lewis, who never said anything except "Don't forget to check the oil in that mower; it'll burn up the engine without it," or "Make sure you sand the steps when you're done shoveling." Directions and orders, but no stories, no jokes, and no talk ever about Mrs. Lewis. There was no reason for Ricky to hang around their house any longer than it took to get the work done and have something to eat or drink. But, over time, he'd gotten used to Mr. Lewis' being so quiet and had learned it was easier to be around him if neither of them talked. So, whenever Ricky finished mowing the lawn, maybe after supper on a summer's evening, he wouldn't say a word as they sat in the rockers on the porch, drinking lemonade made from a can. Instead, he'd watch the sky turn dusky over the garden and listen to the whippoorwills and crickets, keeping his thoughts to himself. Like how he missed her homemade lemonade— the tartness of it, and the pretty wedge of lemon on the edge of the glass.

When he'd gone by the other evening to let Mr. Lewis know he couldn't work at the mill that weekend, the old man had just nodded at the explanation and said, "That's responsibility—letting me know ahead. Otherwise, I would have cooked for two and wasted my time waiting for you. You'd have been out of a job, that'd happened. Understand?"

He'd understood all right. It was a good thing his mother had kept bugging him about letting Mr. Lewis know. If she hadn't hounded him every day about it, he probably wouldn't have gone up there.

· · ■ · ·

Matt got up and looked out the window. "I hate this crappy plastic," he said. "Can't see nothing. I'm gonna wait outside."

Ricky watched him go, then looked over at Katie. She was all dressed up and sitting on the floor beside her pal, her little fingers pulling out the burrs behind Boomer's ears. Although the dog's top lip was quivering and his eyes were winking in pain, he lay there and took it. Ricky knew if it was Matt, or even him, ripping out those burrs, Boomer would have snapped off his fingers. There wasn't anything Katie couldn't do to that dog, but still he told her, "Be easy. You're hurting him."

Katie gave him a wide-eyed look. "Ow-wee," she said and pointed at the dog's ear. "Poor Boomah." She hugged his head, then went back to work.

Perhaps it was that they were going to bury their father in another hour, or that he'd been thinking about Mrs. Lewis since he'd woken up that morning, but watching his baby sister—whose first word wasn't "Momma" or "Dada" but "Boomah"—he suddenly found himself wondering what it was going to do to her when that dog died. It gave him a sick feeling. "Get away from that stinky dog," he snapped at her. "You're going to get yourself all dirty."

Katie gave her brother a wounded look, then a defiant one. "No!" she said.

Just then, their mother walked into the living room, wearing the same black dress she'd worn to the wake and the funeral mass. "You look nice, Ma," he told her.

"Black's never been a good color for me," she said, looking down at her dress. "But it's only right." She picked up Katie and put her on her feet. Brushing off the dog hair, she said, "Time to go bye-bye."

"Boomah come?" asked Katie.

"No," said their mother as she put on Katie's coat. "Boomer has to stay here." She smoothed the hair under Katie's hat. "All ready?"

"Kisses," said Katie, then darted away from her mother's arms to give Boomer a kiss goodbye.

Watching her, Ricky was grateful it was their father they were burying today and not their dog.

.. ■ ..

Although it was sunny, the wind had a bite to it. "So much for curling my hair," said their mother as they headed up the driveway. "You'd think it was March instead of April."

"Which way?" asked Ricky as soon as he maneuvered Katie's carriage onto the tarred surface of Ridge Road. "Long way, or the short way?"

His mother hesitated. "If we take the long way, we don't have to go through town," she said.

It was just what Ricky had been thinking. He didn't want to walk past the general store and have everybody see them. "Yeah," he agreed. "We walk by the store looking like this, they'll think we're going to church or something."

"And Old Biddy Botto will probably run out of her house to tell us Easter was last week," added Matt.

"That would give her something to chew on," said their mother, already heading in the direction of the long way. "That woman's saddest day in life was the day Ma Bell took the party line out of Harmony Center."

"What's that mean?" asked Matt.

"When I was little," their mother explained, "people in certain parts of town were still on the same telephone line, which meant you'd sometimes pick up the phone and hear them talking. You could always tell when someone picked up on you, because you'd hear the click. That woman lived on the horn in those days, waiting for a piece of gossip to put through the rumor mill. But sometimes she'd forget she wasn't supposed to be eavesdropping on everyone else's business, and let an 'oh my' or something like that slip." Their mother ran a hand through her windblown hair, her thin fingers pulling away the strands stuck to the corner of her mouth. "Just remember, boys, what goes around comes around. That meddling old hen's deaf as a doorstop these days."

"Cold," said Katie.

Ricky stopped the carriage and rearranged Katie's "stinky" blanket. He carefully tucked it around her legs, making sure none of its edges were hanging down near the wheels.

"Do you want me to push for a while?" asked his mother, who waited up ahead with Matt.

"Nah, I've got her," said Ricky. He pushed on, feeling restless. Although they were headed in the opposite direction from his usual route, just being on the same road made him want to run. It was an urge that was too hard for him to curb, and, straightening his arms, he began to run behind the carriage, making car noises, his voice revving and shifting gears.

His baby sister started laughing. "Whee," she cried. He passed by Matt and his mother, who warned him, "Not too fast, Ricky. You might hit a bump. She might fall out."

But he was already on his way to the victory line at the Indy 500, his sister's laughter bubbling in his ears like applause. He pushed Katie up the incline by Dan Simmons' run-down mobile home, where two of Dan's little brothers were outside in the dumpy yard playing robber. As soon as they noticed Ricky, both boys aimed their sticks at him, then *k-shooed* him with imaginary bullets. The younger announced, "We got him!"

Ricky's sideways glance traveled past the boys, his eyes scanning the dirty, shaded windows for Dan, a tingling of fear running through him—*Hey, Gordon, where you going?* And what would he say? *None of your beeswax?* Or *Up to Pine Grove to bury our father. Wanna come?* That'd give Dan something to chew on with Bugsie. Like Ma said, what goes around comes around, he thought. One of these days, someone was going to dunk their faces in a toilet full of shit.

He turned away from the windows and hurried up the hill to the country crossroads, where Pine Grove and Ridge Road intersected. Looking to his left, he thought, Least we don't have to go down there. From where he was standing, he could see a big black sign, suspended by chains, rocking in the wind. The sign was shaped like a German shepherd's head, and though he was too far away to make out the gold lettering of McCarthy's Kennels, he was close enough to hear the faint sounds of barking. At school, Bugsie was always bragging about how his father raised attack dogs for policemen, and how if Wavin' Beady had owned one of their dogs he never would have been murdered.

"Doggie," said Katie. She stared up at Ricky, her cheeks red as apples. "Where Boomah?"

"At home," said Ricky, leaning over to fix the frilly bonnet that covered one of her eyes.

"Where Momma?" asked Katie.

"She's coming."

"Where Matt?"

"He's coming, too." Ricky tried to wipe her runny nose with the edge of her blanket, but Katie turned her head. "Where Daddy?" she asked.

The question took Ricky by surprise. It was something she hadn't asked in a long time. "He's all gone," Ricky reminded her. "Now, hold still and let me wipe your nose."

"All gone," said Katie. "Daddy all gone."

When Matt and his mother caught up to them, they turned down Pine Grove and continued on together. The only house between the intersection and where the road ended at the cemetery a mile away was the Lawrences' place.

"I imagine Gloria still has her Easter decorations up," said their mother. "Be nice for Katie to see."

Mrs. Lawrence was seriously into lawn decorating, and her themes rotated with each season and major holiday. At Christmas, no one could compete with her light show, which Ricky's mother liked to say "you could see all the way from Belfast." His father had always said, "Hate to see their 'lectric bill." Besides the lights that outlined their entire house and fence, there was the life-sized Frosty the Snowman, and Santa with his sleigh and reindeer. There was also a herd of elves carrying presents, and a nativity that was bigger than the one outside St. Anne's Catholic Church.

" 'Member the year someone stole one of her Wise Men?" asked Matt. "Diana put up a big *Missing* sign at the store with his picture on it."

"Yeah, I remember," said Ricky. "All the kids at school said we were the ones that took it, and you started bawling on the bus 'cause they were calling us kidnappers and saying, 'Gordon's probably gonna steal Baby Jesus next.' "

"I was only in kindergarten," said Matt defensively, "and I wasn't bawling 'cause of that. I was scared Our Cop was gonna arrest us and make us go to jail like the uncles."

"That's the first time I've heard that," said their mother. "Makes me wonder what else you two never tell me."

Ricky and Matt exchanged guilty looks, then Matt quickly changed the subject. "Hey, look at that!" he said as they approached the Lawrences'. "She's got eggs hanging in her tree this year."

Ricky pointed at the plastic statue in the middle of the yard that was almost as tall as he was. "Look, Katie! There's the Easter Bunny. Must not have had time to fill all his baskets last weekend." But when he looked down, he saw his baby sister was asleep.

"Don't wake her up; I'll bring her by another time," said their mother, leaning over to cover Katie with the blanket. "Look, she's smiling in her sleep."

"Probably dreaming about Boomer," said Matt.

As they started walking again, their mother reached out and draped her arm around Matt. "I need to tell you boys something before we get there," she said.

Ricky looked over at her, the tone of her voice already warning him that it was something important. "What?" he asked.

"I'm not quite sure how to put it," she said, then looked down at the potholed road, as though the words she was looking for were hiding in the broken asphalt.

"Even though now it's hard for me to remember why," she finally said, "I loved your father once. . . . I guess what I'm trying to say is that, when we bury him today, I'm going to try and remember something good about him."

She stopped walking and stared at them. "I want you boys to try and do that, too," she said, the wind running through her hair like invisible fingers. "The way I figure it, it's not right to bury someone with nothing but hate in your heart. When you're as old as me, you'll understand that."

Ricky stared down at his red hands holding on to the carriage, trying to make sense of what she'd said, and why he suddenly felt so mad. He looked up at the sky, watching a cloud pass by the sun, its shadow making the wind seem even colder.

"He took me to the fair once," said Matt, so softly Ricky barely heard him above the gusty, whistling wind. "Bought me blue cotton candy, and let me ride the Ferris wheel four times."

"Then that's what you should remember," said their mother as they started walking again. "Something good like that."

· · ■ · ·

Matt had told Ricky on several occasions that the day they buried their father he was going to piss on his grave. But Matt didn't, he cried instead. Ricky figured it was because he was remembering the time their father had taken him to the fair. He figured his mother cried because she was remembering how she'd loved him once. But the tears Ricky shed were for someone else. Though he'd tried his best to remember something good about his father while Father Bob was saying those prayers, all he could think of was the person who'd always been good to him. As he stood there in the cold wind, all the pictures in his head were of Mrs. Lewis. He saw her at the floury kitchen table, rolling dough and wearing her red apron with the yellow flowers on it; then outside, feeding and talking to her birds. He saw her rubbing her chin as she studied a hand of cards, her white hair shining and those smiling blue eyes looking at him through silver-rimmed glasses. He saw those brown-spotted hands that had never touched him with anything but love.

The graveside service was a short one. It was over before he'd even gotten used to seeing that casket again, before his baby sister ever woke up.

Their mother hadn't wanted the burial to be a circus, and it wasn't. There was no Aunt June howling like a dog, no uncles in chains, no one there to watch them cry except for Father Bob, and Mr. Lewis.

·· ■ ··

Although he was exhausted that night, Ricky couldn't fall asleep. Stretched out on the couch, he watched the watery moon through the plastic, his mind churning the day over and over. The bacon at breakfast. His mother's story about Old Biddy Botto. Katie's laughter as he'd raced her carriage up the hill. It wasn't the graveside service or the final last look at his father's casket that was holding on to him. It was the journey to Pine Grove Cemetery: them walking the long way through the wind together; his baby sister saying "Daddy all gone" while he was standing at the crossroads; the way that cloud had passed across the sun.

"Ricky?"

He turned his head, and, staring through the darkness, saw Matt's white T-shirt glowing with moonlight. "What?"

"You awake?"

"I'm talking to you, ain't I? What's the matter?"

"I'm scared."

"The field mice scratching in the walls again?"

"Not that," said Matt, sitting down on the edge of the couch. "I'm scared Ma's gonna die and they'll put her in one of those boxes, too, and we'll never see her again."

Ricky could feel his brother shivering, and gave him some of his blanket. "Don't think bad things like that," he said. "Besides, look at Mrs. Wilson—she's almost a hundred and still grows her own tomatoes."

"I can't help it," said Matt. "My brain won't stop thinking about it. I keep 'membering how he used to say, 'If you little bastards don't straighten out you'll be living in a foster home.' 'Member that?"

" 'I'm gonna pack your clothes right now,' " said Ricky, imitating their father's voice. Sometimes his father would pick up the phone and pretend he was talking to the foster home—"How soon can I bring him over?" and stuff like that—and once he'd even made Ricky pack up his clothes in a grocery bag and take them out to the truck.

"Nothing but another one of his lies," Ricky said firmly. "He never would've let us live in one of those foster places 'cause they'd stop giving him food stamps and welfare and make him get a job—that's what Aunt Donna said when I asked her about it. She said he just said that to scare me. I've only told you that about a hundred times."

"I know, but if Ma died they might make us live in

one of those places," said Matt in a teary voice. "And you, me, and Katie might not get to be in the same one, like that one kid and his sister I saw on TV."

"You keep dreaming up this kind of stuff, Ma's going to make you go see that shrink lady twice a week instead of just Tuesdays," Ricky told him. "If anything ever happened to Ma, which it ain't, we'd live with Aunt Donna and Aunt Lane over the shop. And there's no way they'd ever split us up. So don't be worrying about things that won't happen."

Matt sat in the dark, mulling it over. "You're right. Aunt Donna and Aunt Lane would take us. But I bet Aunt Lane wouldn't let us bring Boomer. Cripe, she's ascared of little poodles."

"Go to bed, Matt," said Ricky, who could now barely keep his eyes open. "I need my sleep for running."

But Matt wasn't listening. "Katie couldn't live without Boomer," he said.

"All right," Ricky told him. "I'll sleep in our room with you, but just for tonight, you hear?"

"Thanks, Ricky. I promise I won't wet the bed. I haven't drank any water since supper, and I used the bathroom before I woke you up."

"That's good," said Ricky, but, despite Matt's promise, he left his blanket behind on the couch to keep it dry. He followed his little brother down the dark hall to their room, where the Jesus night-light glowed against the wall. He hadn't slept in there for some time, since he felt better in the morning when he slept in the living room. He'd also noticed through the graphs he'd

110

been making that his times were always faster if he wasn't up with Matt in the middle of the night changing sheets. In his log he'd written: "good sleep = faster time."

He crawled across their lumpy bed to his side and settled under the covers, which smelled of Lysol. Matt rearranged his fry pan, then curled up beside him.

For a while Ricky listened to the wind outside, sucking and wrinkling the plastic on their bedroom window. There were other familiar night noises, too—the water tapping in the bathroom sink; Boomer whining for a few seconds in a dog dream; the loud hum of the refrigerator in the kitchen. When he finally heard the sound he was waiting for—Matt's slow, steady, breathing—he closed his eyes and drifted off to sleep.

Chapter Eight

Not including April vacation, it took Ricky twenty-one weekdays and forty-two tries to run the whole route without having to jog. During that time, things were changing. The clocks had been turned ahead an hour, and now it was light out till after seven-thirty. Mud season was finally over, the grass was turning green, and the crocuses and daffodils had already bloomed. Ricky had noticed, too, that the pair of mallards had returned to the Bakers' farm pond. Mothers were hanging laundry outside again and fathers were cleaning up their yards.

A lot had happened during the days and weeks since Ricky began running instead of jogging. He'd had that close call with Bugsie and his boys in the bathroom at school. On Easter Sunday, for the first time that he could ever remember, his family had enjoyed a holiday without a fight. And on April 29, 119 days after their father was killed driving home drunk, they'd buried his body in Pine Grove Cemetery.

Although those were the major events, it was the minor ones recorded in Ricky's running notebook that perhaps revealed more crucial changes in his life. For example, the day he'd run down Ridge Road barefoot through the puddles and rain, he'd written in his log: "running = fun." It had been a surprise to him to see that equation: up until that point, he'd only thought of running as a way to beat the bus.

There were other things that he'd discovered as a result of notations in his running log that altered his life in small ways. For one, he'd learned that if he ate breakfast before he ran he always got a stomachache, but when he didn't eat he couldn't think straight by math class. To solve that problem, he became a Breakfast Eater again. It wasn't easy joining Matt and the other little kids in the cafeteria, but, the way Ricky looked at it, he didn't have a choice—if he wanted to run without feeling sick and still be able to think during math, he needed to eat well and at a certain time. Still, that first week it was hard for him to ignore the embarrassed looks from his peers, and Bugsie's cutting "Hey, look, it's the Champion of Breakfast Eaters." But by the second week, it felt so good to sit in class without having his stomach growl and his head ache that he no longer cared what the others thought or said about it. Besides, as Matt put it to his friends, "My brother's in training, he has to eat."

It was also through his running graphs that Ricky had discovered his morning times were always slower than those in the afternoon, and that both times were always slower on rainy days and Mondays. There was nothing he could do about the weather, but he figured that if he ran on weekends he wouldn't feel as tired on Mondays. So he began getting up on Saturdays and Sundays at the usual time, but instead of running to school, he ran different routes. Twice he'd taken the old logging road just past McCarthy's Kennels, and followed it to the back side of Loon Lake. Another time he'd run all the way to the train trestle up by Dead Man's Curve, where he'd stopped long enough to look down the steep embankment at the place where his father's truck had crashed into the trees.

But the route he liked best was the long way up to Pine Grove Cemetery. From there he made the loop through town, past the store, the mill, and the fire station. At St. Anne's Church he turned left onto Mountain Road, which made the last leg home fast and easy, since it was all downhill. During April vacation, he'd run that route each morning before his mother left for work, and each afternoon when she got home. And that was when the mill men—who always ate breakfast and lunch at the general store, and who usually congregated there again in the afternoons, right after the mill's four-thirty whistle blew—began to notice him.

"Heard Jim Garvey said he's a real whiz kid in math."

"Runs to school every day, and during that freak snowstorm Lafayette said he had to beg him before he'd take a ride."

"Works like a dog for the old man on Saturday mornings, I can tell you that; he's the one that straightened out the drawers in the drill-bit bin, and he's why the toilet in the can's always clean on Mondays."

Although Ricky had noticed that drivers never passed him now without waving or honking their horns, and that men putting in overtime on Saturdays down at the mill had started calling him "Ricky" instead of "Hey, kid," he was unaware of what was being said about him around town.

He was also unaware that the most important entry he'd made in his running log during that time was the two sentences he'd copied from a book he'd found in the school library: "Long-distance runners are often solitary, quiet, and stoic. They have great stamina and resistance to pain."

Beneath the quote, Ricky had jotted down definitions of the words that were unfamiliar to him, having looked them up in Mrs. Parker's classroom dictionary. The book's description of a long-distance runner appealed to him, for he saw himself in some of those words. He was solitary because he ran alone, and because, except for Lyle, he had no friends. Although he wasn't sure he understood the definition of "stoic," which was "unaffected by pleasure or pain," he figured any kid his age had to be brave to be a Breakfast Eater. He was definitely quiet, and he had to have stamina to run seven miles a day. For the first time in his life, Ricky began to identify himself as being something other than a "Gordon."

But this Wednesday morning in the third week of May, Ricky wasn't thinking about any of that as he started running down Ridge Road. He was focused instead on time, on the cheap digital watch in the palm of his hand—a Happy Meal prize that his brother had given him last night when Aunt Donna had brought him home from his weekly visit with Dr. Munsen.

Ricky had never known how fast he ran the route until he reached home or school and checked the clock on the stove or the one in his classroom, but now he'd be able to keep track of his time while he was actually running. This possibility excited him and made him run even faster. Each time he passed a landmark, he looked down at the watch and made a mental note of how long it had taken him to reach it. While his body raced against the watch, his mind raced as well. Time was an amazing thing. He figured it was the only thing everyone in the whole world had in common: a second was a second whether you lived in China, or some jungle in Africa, or Harmony Center, Maine. Time was something that was always moving forward; it never stopped even if the battery in your watch died or the power went out in a storm. Time was the only thing between him and beating the bus.

.. ■ ..

"Did the watch help?" asked Matt as he put his breakfast tray down on the table at school.

"It was great," said Ricky. "Look at this." He turned his notebook around so his brother could see the graph he'd been working on. "From these times here, I'll be able to see where I'm the slowest. Remember when Mr. Lafayette gave me a ride when we had that snowstorm? Well, while he was yapping about how I could get killed and all, I kept watching his odometer. That's how I was able to break down the route from the Denisons' to school by actual miles, and . . ."

"You gonna eat your sausage?" Matt interrupted. "Or is that another thing that ain't good for you anymore?"

"You can have it," Ricky told him, slightly irritated. Here he was trying to explain to his brother why the Happy Meal watch was so valuable and all Matt cared about was getting to eat his sausage. "Do you want me to show you this or not?"

"I don't care about that math stuff," Matt told him. "I just wanted to know if the watch helped."

Ricky looked at his little brother, knowing it was useless. Matt didn't love numbers like he did. Like his brother's blue eyes, it was a difference between them. "It helped a lot," said Ricky.

"Hey, look," said Matt, pointing at Sonny Wells, who had a plastic tray in his hand and was looking for a place to sit. "What's he doing here?"

Ricky was wondering the same thing as he watched

the sixth-grader set his tray down at their table. "Mind if I sit here?" asked Sonny.

"Free country," said Matt.

"Thanks," Sonny said, his face as red as the plastic tray. "I didn't want to sit with the babies." He slid in beside Ricky, giving him a shy look and an explanation. "I'm in training," he said, nodding at his tray. "Baseball."

"Yeah," Ricky agreed. "You gotta eat breakfast when you're in training."

"But you shouldn't eat sausage," Matt told him. "It's not good for you, right, Ricky?"

"I don't know about baseball players," said Ricky, "but I read it's not good for runners." Seeing the disappointed look on Sonny's face, Ricky added, "You can eat those eggs, though, 'cause they're scrambled, not fried, and the banana's great for you; it has a lot of potassium."

Sonny scanned his tray, then Matt's. "I'll trade you my sausage for your banana," he told him.

"Deal," said Matt. "I'm not in training for nothing."

·· ■ ··

That afternoon it was so hot out that Ricky wished he had shorts on. Running down Ridge Road, he felt like his backpack had bricks in it, and his sweaty legs, which were sticking to and chafing against his jeans, felt like lead. By the time he reached the Bakers' farm pond, his scalp prickled with sweat and the skin beneath his damp clothes crawled with imaginary bugs. Although the temptation to dive right into that brown water was powerful, the watch cupped in his hand kept him moving.

It felt like the middle of July as he ran down that tarred road, his feet burning inside his worn-out socks and black shoes. There wasn't even a breeze in the sticky air, which felt so heavy in his chest that his shallow breathing sounded to him like Lyle's. His mouth was so dry his tongue felt like it was growing and taking up so much space he could hardly swallow air. He wasn't used to running in weather like this, which had brought out the clouds of black flies that were swarming around his head and making a meal of him. The tips of both ears, his neck, and the corner of one eye were already swollen and dotted with blood.

He glanced down at the watch in his hand. The seconds seemed to tick inside him like the throbbing heartbeat in his cheeks, making him want to keep on going though his body was ready to give up—his throat was screaming for water, the muscles in his rubbery legs were quivering. Like that morning when the snow had fallen so thick and fast it had blinded him— like all those times he had run in the bone-chilling cold or pouring rain—he could now feel his will giving in. His brain was starting to turn against him, *Why?* and *Who cares?* already slowing him down. Although his feet were still moving, the desire was slipping away from him, that new image of himself as a long-distance runner melting away in the heat. He gripped the watch so tightly he could feel its edges cutting into his fingers and tried to fight off the urge to quit by silently chanting, "stamina, stamina, stamina."

He rounded the bend by the Beady property, and the battle inside his head stopped as abruptly as his feet did. Leaning over to catch his breath, he stared at the blue Chevy in the driveway, and then at Our Cop, who was standing in the middle of the front yard, staring at the ground like he was still searching for clues. For weeks last fall, the State Police and those detectives from Bangor had crawled all over that yard, their unmarked cars always in the driveway when the bus passed by. But the detectives never arrested anyone, and after they'd packed up all their stuff and left Harmony Center empty-handed, the only car Ricky ever saw in that driveway was Our Cop's.

But it wasn't seeing the blue Chevy in the driveway or Our Cop standing in the yard that had caused Ricky to stop running. It was the For Sale sign. When did they put that up? he wondered. It hadn't been there that morning; he would have noticed it.

Ricky wiped his eyes with the edge of his T-shirt, then started to walk closer, noticing that the police ribbon and stakes were gone and that someone had raked the lawn. A pile of dead leaves and branches squatted by the side of the house like a bush.

"What you stopping for, Ricky?" Our Cop called over to him. "Don't you have a bus to beat?"

Ricky glanced down at the watch in his hand. "Not today," he said with a defeated sigh. "It's too hot; I ain't used to it yet." He stopped by the front walk. Even though the ribbon was gone, he didn't dare go in the yard.

"I'm not used to it, either," said Our Cop. He stepped around the For Sale sign as though it had teeth and might bite him, and, patting at his forehead with a folded handkerchief, walked over to Ricky. "Feels like August," he said. "Think we're in for a dry summer. You'll have to be careful cooking your beans in the woods up on Hatchet Mountain."

Ricky smiled—it figured Our Cop knew about that. There wasn't much that happened in Harmony Center that he didn't know. As town constable, his job also included running the town dump, so he even knew what people around there threw away in their trash. Ricky had heard the men down at the store making fun of the thin man standing beside him for as far back as he could remember. They called him the Trashmaster, and said stuff like, "Only thing Our Cop ever has to shoot at is the rats down at the dump." But it was Our Cop's number that Ricky had always dialed when his family needed to be rescued from his drunken father. It was the blue flashing light on the dash of that Chevy that he'd watched and prayed for in the dark while he waited at the end of the driveway, crying and petrified that help wouldn't get there in time to save his mother, his brother, his baby sister. Our Cop knew more about him than cooking beans in the woods with Matt. He'd seen Ricky in his underwear bawling like a baby. He'd seen the inside of that broken house too many times to count.

"How's your family doing?" Our Cop asked him.

"Good," said Ricky. Now *he's* buried, we're doing even better—Matt's only wetting the bed once or twice a week, he added silently.

"Your mother's working for Cindy Chaffee, isn't she?"

"Yup," said Ricky. Over *his* dead body. "She says after we get a car again, she wants to go back to school so she can make more money." 'Cause *he* didn't leave us nothing but bills and a car that doesn't work.

"Tell her I'll keep my eye out for her. If I hear of anyone selling a car, I'll let her know."

"Thanks," said Ricky, staring at the Realtor sign, his mind automatically memorizing the telephone number on it. No matter how big that house was, or that it had a barn and lots of land, Ricky would rather live in his dump down the road than in the place where Wavin' Beady had been murdered. "They're gonna sell it, huh?"

Our Cop turned around and stared back at the sign as though he couldn't believe it either. "Shame, really," he said. "Been in their family four generations. But I can see their side of it."

"Who'd buy it?" Ricky wondered out loud.

"Oh, someone will, I expect," said Our Cop. "Probably some out-of-stater, looking for a summer house up-country. I'll end up having to watch it in the winter for them while they're down in Florida playing golf; be calling me up every time we get a snowstorm on the national news, just like the rest of them flatlanders on Loon Lake."

Gazing up at the empty windows, Ricky asked something he'd wondered about almost every time he sprinted by this house. "Think they'll ever catch him? I mean the murderer?"

Our Cop's gray eyes studied him for a moment, then looked back at the yard. "Justice has a way of catching up to people, Ricky. Whoever did that to Roland Beady will pay for it somewhere down the line, I can promise you that."

"Yeah, maybe," said Ricky. After all, justice had caught up to his father on Dead Man's Curve. *The driver, William Gordon, of Harmony Center, was decapitated when his body was ejected from the vehicle.* A fact that Our Cop hadn't told them that morning when he'd come to their house to break the news, but one Ricky had learned while reading the newspaper. *Authorities believe speed and alcohol were a factor. . . .*

The sound of the approaching bus caused them both to turn, and they watched in silence as it sped by, all the kids in the windows pointing at them or the sign, Ricky wasn't sure which.

"A-r-r-e-s-s-t h-i-i-i-m-m-m," trailed a voice that Ricky recognized as Bugsie's.

Although they both knew who Bugsie was referring to, Our Cop said, "I should. He drives that bus like a bat out of hell." He watched the yellow vehicle disappear around the bend, then looked at Ricky. "You want a ride home? I'm heading that way."

Ricky glanced at the car in the driveway. It was tempting—he was sweating like a pig, and today's race was already over. "Thanks," he said, "but I gotta get used to running in the heat sometime."

"Wish I could have an ounce of that spirit," said Our Cop, staring at that pile of brush by the side of the house. "Think everyone in this town could use some."

Ricky wasn't sure what Our Cop was talking about, but the defeated look in those gray eyes was one he recognized. He'd seen it every time Our Cop had tried to talk his mother into pressing charges. "See you," said Ricky, suddenly feeling uncomfortable. "I'd better get running."

"Don't let me hold you up," Our Cop told him, shifting his gaze away from the yard, where any clues that might have gone unnoticed way back in November had long since been washed away by the weather, or were now raked away by some Realtor from Belfast. "Just tell your mother what I said about the car. And if she needs anything, you know my number, right?"

Ricky nodded, thinking, You kidding? First one I ever learned.

He took off running, looking over his shoulder only once, as he neared the bend. Our Cop was still standing where he'd left him, watching the house as though waiting for it to answer the question that everyone in Harmony Center was still asking. Right after Wavin'

Beady had been murdered, people thought it had to have been done by a stranger, someone just passing through town. But as the weeks passed and no stranger had been caught, people started looking at their neighbors instead. Ricky had heard his father tell his mother that it might have been Duckmaker having one of his Vietnam flashbacks. He'd said Duckmaker probably saw Roland out there waving and thought he was throwing a grenade.

As rumors about who it could have been began to circulate, kids on the bus and at school repeated what they overheard. *If those Gordon brothers weren't already in prison.... He has a wicked temper when he's drinking.... Put his wife in the hospital before; busted her cheekbone and broke her nose.... Our Cop's down at their house at least three nights a week breaking up fights.*

Although there was some truth in those cruel rumors, Ricky knew for certain it wasn't his father that had killed Wavin' Beady—he'd been so falling-down drunk that weekend he'd never even gotten off the couch. Still, it was the Wise Man thing all over again, only worse. All the kids had whispered about them. Mrs. Benson had made up excuses about Lyle being too busy or sick to have Ricky over. He'd had to defend himself and Matt against the lies and bits of truth the only way he knew how—with his fists. He'd been in and out of Daniels' office like a yo-yo.

Seeing Our Cop at Wavin' Beady's had resurrected those painful memories, and they jabbed at him as he ran down Ridge Road. Didn't matter if it was stealing a

Wise Man or killing an old man or if some kids at school were sent home because of bugs; if your last name was Gordon, you were the one who stole it, or murdered him, or gave them cooties. Couldn't even stand on his own road without some kid like Bugsie yelling, "Arrest him!"

Ricky was sick of being blamed for everything and anything that went wrong in this town. He was sick of the whispers and the looks and the way they said the name "Gordon" as though he were nothing but garbage. His mother was right; even with his father dead and buried they were still paying for his sins. It wasn't fair, and as his feet kept on moving he could feel the anger of that injustice boiling inside him. By the time he reached his driveway, where Matt and Boomer were waiting, the sweat was running into his eyes and dripping off his nose.

"What took you so long?" asked Matt, getting to his feet. "I'm dying of thirst. I was about ready to go down to the porch and drink out of Boomer's bowl."

Ricky staggered to a stop and threw off his backpack. It hit the ground with a thud.

Matt picked it up for him. "What you got in here? Rocks?"

Ricky shoved the watch in his pocket without looking at the numbers, then ripped off his drenched T-shirt. Boomer picked up the shirt in his mouth and started prancing down the driveway like he'd gotten himself a groundhog or a mole. "Get back here, dog!"

ordered Ricky, but Boomer pranced on, the shirt wagging in his mouth like a dead body.

"Gonna put it in his mole pile, probably," Matt said, laughing, then looked at Ricky. "Let's go. The black flies are eatin' me. Cripe, I pulled off three ticks just waiting for you."

Although Matt's nightmares and bed-wetting had been getting better, he still didn't dare to go in the house by himself. "Don't blame the ticks and being thirsty on me," snapped Ricky. "You could have gone in the house instead of sitting out here like a wussy baby."

Matt threw Ricky's backpack at him, his blue eyes like chips of ice. "Carry it yourself, asshole."

Whatever it was that'd been building inside him back there on the hot road finally exploded. Ricky left the backpack where it landed and started to chase Matt down the driveway, their father's favorite saying coming out of his mouth like a growl: "I'm gonna get you!"

Matt made it to the porch before Ricky did but didn't go inside the house. Instead, he cowered beneath one of the windows, his arms covering his head as he waited for the blows. Ricky took one look at his brother and saw himself waiting for the mop handle to land, its flash of blue coming down on his shoulders, the back of his neck, over and over. *Talk back to me, you little bastard! I'll show you who's boss.* Coming down on him till he just lay there in a heap, looking up at that foggy window. He was nine years old and had made the mistake of telling his father that his "thrifty man's storm windows" were nothing but plastic. He'd repeated without thinking what the kids at school had said: "That's a white-trash way of keeping warm."

"You hit me and I'm gonna call Our Cop on you," Matt yelled.

But Ricky never heard the warning; his frazzled mind was on something else. He walked over to where Matt was crouched and started to tear away the plastic that was fastened to the window above his brother's head. His fingers furrowed along the edges of the wood, pulling and yanking till the rusty staples began to give, the plastic making a popping sound as he ripped it away from the casing.

Matt unfolded himself and inched out of the way. "You gone nuts or something, Ricky?" he asked, the anger in his voice now replaced with worry. "Someone say something bad at school?"

Without his brother beneath the window, Ricky had more leverage. He took two fistfuls of the stiff, slippery material and, leaning backward, used his weight to pull. He grunted and yanked, and staples started flying back at him, the glass beneath the plastic revealing itself, the room inside where he'd taken that beating becoming clearer with each tug.

His fingers latched on to another edge of plastic, just above the sill. Turning his body, he pulled like a draft horse, his feet digging against the porch, his bare shoulders taking the brunt of the strain. More staples shot into the air like bullets. Others held to the wood, the plastic tearing around them as Ricky heaved and grunted, the muscles in his arms burning with the effort of prying the "storm windows" free. Suddenly the tug-of-war was over and he stumbled forward, the plastic fanning around him like a cape. He let go of it, turning to watch it float like a foggy cloud to the floor of the porch.

Panting, Ricky looked over at Matt. "We don't need this shit no more," he said, and he wasn't just referring to the plastic or their father. "We're done being this town's white trash."

Matt stared down at the layer of plastic, then kicked at it with his shoe. "Yeah," he said with understanding. "No one's better than us."

Ricky grinned at his brother. "Come on!" he told him. "Let's tear it all down."

Matt let out a yell like a warrior going into battle, then bolted toward the next window, with Ricky right behind him. They both attacked the plastic, tearing and tugging, laughing as they tore the staples free.

Chapter Nine

Ricky maneuvered the lawn mower around the garden that he'd helped to plant in Mr. Lewis' yard. Even in the fading light, he could already see that the peas and onions were coming up. When he finished the last section, he turned off the mower and pushed it up to the barn but didn't put it inside. He wouldn't until it was stone-cold, or Mr. Lewis would chew him out good about how it could start a fire.

As he walked toward the front porch, he surveyed the lawn with a critical eye and felt a sense of satisfaction. The grass was so even and neat; the dandelions would be gone for a few more days.

Mr. Lewis was sitting in his rocker on the porch, sucking on a pipe, the thin threads of smoke mingling with the scent of freshly cut grass. Before he had the chance to ask, Ricky told him, "I didn't put the mower in the barn."

Mr. Lewis gave a nod of approval, then said, "Lemonade's in the fridge; cookies on the counter; help yourself."

Ricky didn't bother to take any of the store-bought cookies, but he returned with two glasses. "Here you go." He handed one to Mr. Lewis, then sat down on the porch swing and stared at the empty rocker where Mrs. Lewis used to sit on warm nights like this. While he was mowing, he'd seen a cardinal perched on the sundial, and if Mrs. Lewis was still alive he would have told her about it. Instead, he just sat there sipping on his watery drink, keeping his thoughts to himself as usual. It was after eight, but still light enough to see how nice the lawn looked beneath the graying sky, and it made him think of his own yard down the road. It had come a long way since that day he and Matt went kind of crazy and tore down every one of those "thrifty man's storm windows." It had felt so good getting rid of the plastic that he and Matt wanted to get rid of all of *him*—the beer cans and broken bottles, the litter of cigarette butts ground into the dirt, the rusty tools that'd been left outside so long they were good for nothing. For the past three weeks they'd been working on the yard almost every day after school. They'd rolled all the dead tires into the woods out back, where no one could see them, and bagged up all the trash. Then they'd raked the dirt free of glass and mowed what little grass there was all the way to the trees.

Seeing the work they'd done, their mother had started fixing things up, too. She'd washed all the windows and made pretty curtains for the living room. She'd even had Mr. Finks haul away the Ford truck that'd been living in their yard without an engine or wheels for years. He'd taken it away for free, saying that what he'd make selling its doors and radio and the bed on the back would cover the cost of hauling it to the junkyard. As Matt put it, "Our yard's so clean, Boomer goes in the woods to take his dumps now."

Looking down at his glass, which was still full, Mr. Lewis said, "This lemonade's awful."

You put too many cans of water in it, thought Ricky, but only said, "At least it's cold."

"Can't make it from scratch like she could," Mr. Lewis admitted. "I miss that, and the way she used to put that slice of lemon on the lip of the glass. Like having the sun smile at you when you took a drink."

"Yeah," Ricky agreed. "No one could make cinnamon-oatmeal cookies like her either." He looked toward the side lawn, at her village of birdhouses, feeling a tightness inside of him. Although she'd died over a year ago, this was the first time they'd ever talked about her. It gave him a queer feeling, like he was skating on thin ice down at Loon Lake, the surface cracking and creaking and him unsure how far out he dared to go. Still, he took the chance. "I miss everything about her," he said softly.

Mr. Lewis stared down at the glass in his hand, looking somehow older and sadder. His upper lip quivered, and his voice was shaky as he said, "Me, too."

It almost sounded like Mr. Lewis might start crying. Feeling both surprised and embarrassed, Ricky turned away, thinking, *It's as hard for him as it is for me.*

Automatically, Ricky's gaze rested on the green rocker between them. *Best cure for the blues is a bowl of strawberry ice cream with a side order of hugs,* was what she'd probably say. But she was no longer there to give them comfort or to fill the silence with her compliments. There was no Mrs. Lewis now to help them learn to know or like each other, or to make excuses for them. *My husband doesn't wear his heart on his shirtsleeve, but his actions are better than words.* She was no longer there, and yet he could still hear her voice inside his head. *Like it or not, you two are cut from the same Yankee cloth.*

Mr. Lewis cleared his throat as though he had a tickle in it, not tears, and Ricky knew the conversation was over. That "Me, too," had worn them both out. He sighed, then relaxed against the swing, his body feeling pleasantly tired. In the deepening twilight he could hear the music of crickets and peepers, could smell the perfume of cut grass and purple lilacs, could see Mr. Lewis staring out at those birdhouses. As he watched the old man's shadowy figure, sitting straight and still as a statue, it occurred to him for the first time that Mrs. Lewis might have been right. Maybe they were cut from the same Yankee cloth, for, in a way, Mr. Lewis was a long-distance runner, too.

He was certainly quiet: he didn't talk except to give orders or directions. He had great stamina, too, for, though he'd already had a heart attack and was almost eighty, he still worked six days out of seven at the mill. Plus, thought Ricky, he's solitary—living in this big house all by himself. Nobody ever comes over except for me, to shovel and mow and to have breakfast with him on Saturday mornings. He has no one but me to drink his awful lemonade, or, like tonight, to miss Mrs. Lewis with.

And suddenly it was as clear to Ricky as that quarter-moon rising in the evening sky that the "friend of the family" who'd paid for his father's funeral was sitting on the porch with him.

·· ■ ··

The next morning, as Ricky ran by Mr. Lewis' house, he wondered once again why a man who wouldn't even buy himself a new car or heat his whole house would pay for a Gordon's funeral. It made him think about the night before. How sad Mr. Lewis had sounded when he'd said "Me, too," and how old he'd looked sitting there, the sky turning dusky with just a splash of red left above the tree line. I hope Mr. Lewis don't die on me, too, he thought, and it made him feel guilty for wishing all those times that it'd been him instead of her.

Just as Ricky passed the two-mile mark by Wavin' Beady's, he heard a car behind him and veered from the center of the road to the shoulder. As the vehicle got closer, he glanced back at it, expecting the driver to pass, but a red car he didn't recognize slowed down instead. What's he doing? thought Ricky. He glanced back a second time, his eyes focusing briefly on the license plate, then made a waving gesture with his hand that said, *Pass me!*

Over the course of those months since he'd been running, Ricky had come to think of Ridge Road as his private property and cars and trucks as trespassers, especially in the morning, when there were so few of them he could run in the middle of the road. So at first he was irritated when the car didn't pass him and mumbled a few swear words under his breath. But after almost a minute of listening to the hum of that motor creeping behind him, he started getting scared instead. He knew who owned every car, truck, and minivan in Harmony Center. He even knew everyone's license plate—it was a game he liked to play. But he didn't know anyone who had a red station wagon or a 4208YY Maine plate.

Instinctively, Ricky picked up his pace, and his imagination ran away with him. What if it's *him*? he thought, his hands growing sweaty, his arms pumping faster. What if he's come back to kill someone else— say, some kid running along the side of the road all by himself? There was no one else around; no houses close enough for someone to hear a scream or a call for help. They wouldn't even know he was missing until one of the secretaries phoned his mother. *Mrs. Gordon, your son Ricky's not in school today, and we were just wondering if you forgot to call us; is he home sick?* By the time they started looking for him, he'd already be dead in some ditch with a family of crows pecking at his body and eating his eyeballs for lunch.

The adrenaline started rushing through him like a freight train. His fear fed his energy; his feet barely touched the ground between strides. By the time he reached Slowpoke Clara's he was sprinting. For a fleeting second he considered running up her driveway, banging on her front door for help. But he kept on going, knowing that the murderer, who was so close that Ricky could hear a whispered ticking in the engine, would drag him into his car and be down the road before Slowpoke ever got around to opening the door.

Ricky was running for his life, and he ran so fast the duct tape started to unfurl from one of his shoes. If he'd been looking at his watch his rate would have pleased him, but the only thought in his head was *If I make it to the school woods, he can't follow me.*

To Ricky's surprise, when he took a right onto Route 26, the car suddenly took a left and went the other way. Although it was no longer behind him, he couldn't slow down. He didn't dare stop to rest until he finally made it to the swings on the playground.

Hair and clothes lathered with sweat, eyes red with salt, he held on to one of the swings to steady himself and, leaning over, tried to catch his breath. Only now that he believed he was finally safe could he feel the burning sensation in his shivering thighs and the charley horses in his calves. His heart hammered against his aching ribs, and his lungs felt like they were on fire.

"Keep moving, son!"

Ricky lifted his head and saw a man walking toward him. The red station wagon was parked by the sidewalk.

"After a run like that you have to walk or jog some!" the man barked like an order. "Have to help your body cool down!"

Ricky glanced quickly around the empty playground. Run for the building, he told himself; let Daniels know there's a murderer on his premises.

"Come on," said the man, who was taller than Mr. Garvey and now only ten yards away. "We'll walk around the parking lot."

No way! Ricky let go of the swing, prepared to bolt.

Seeming to sense Ricky's fear, the man halted. He held up one hand like a stop sign, then introduced himself. "I'm Mr. Radke. I'm a teacher over at the high school in Belfast, where you'll be going to school in a few years. I'm also the track coach."

Track coach? thought Ricky, noticing the man's windbreaker and the stopwatch around his neck.

"You're Ricky Gordon, right?"

Ricky gave a wary nod, wondering, How's he know my name?

"I've been hearing about you. Wanted to watch you run for myself. Tell me, do you always go that fast?"

Only when a murderer's chasing me, thought Ricky, but he said, "Yeah."

"Keep that up and we'll be good friends when you get to high school."

Ricky was still nervous. He wasn't sure if he trusted this man. That stopwatch could be fake. Murderers liked to trick kids. Oprah had a whole show on it. His mind was already spinning with how he'd get away and tell Our Cop that license-plate number he'd memorized, when, to his great relief, he spotted Mrs. Bourque.

"How have you been, Fred?" she called as she walked toward them from the teachers' parking lot. "Out scouting talent, I see."

Guess he really is a track coach, thought Ricky, watching the two exchange smiles. Good thing I didn't run into Daniels' office yelling *Murderer!*

Mr. Radke's smile grew broader. "Well, Jenny," he said, "they didn't steer me wrong. He sure can run."

"That's not all he's good at," said Mrs. Bourque. "Talk to Jim Garvey—he has him doing junior-high math. Right, Ricky?"

Ricky nodded, thinking, I hope she doesn't tell him about my other grades.

·· ■ ··

"No kidding," said Ricky. "I thought he was the guy that killed Wavin' Beady. I've never run that fast before."

138

"And he's really gonna buy you a new pair of sneakers?" asked Matt, looking toward his classroom.

"Yeah. He said shoes are the most important piece of equipment a runner has. Said I'd end up getting foot problems wearing these ones." Ricky looked down at his Goodwill specials, which for the past week had been held together with duct tape.

"So what's he want?" asked Matt, then added one of their father's sayings: " 'No one gives you somethin' for nothin'.' "

"Just for me to keep running."

"That's it?"

"Buying me shoes is like an investment for him— that's what he said."

"I don't know what that means," said Matt, "but maybe, if you tell him you got a little brother, he'll buy me a pair, too."

Ricky didn't hear this; he was thinking. "I'm glad we cleaned up the yard; least I won't have to worry about him stepping in dog shit. He said he's gonna stop by and talk to Ma tonight."

"Cripe, with a new pair of sneakers you'll beat the bus for sure," said Matt. "Thought you were gonna do it yesterday. Didja hear all the kids yelling?"

Ricky smiled at the memory of those cheers: *Go, Ricky, go!* "I would have beat it this morning," he said. "I was flying. 'Sides, school don't get out till next Wednesday."

"You'll do it," said Matt. "I got a whole buck riding on it."

Ricky was way off his time that afternoon. Running so hard in the morning had taken it out of him. Still, he didn't feel discouraged. He concentrated on some of the pointers the coach had given him. "Keep your elbows bent more and closer to your sides." "Don't run with your chin on your chest, it's harder to breathe." "Before you start running, *always* stretch out first. Your body's like a car; you need to warm it up before you start driving."

Although Mr. Radke had stayed there talking with him until the buses arrived, Ricky had only dared to ask him one question, something that had been bothering him for the past week. He'd pulled out one of his graphs to show the coach the plotted line that had stayed level for four days in a row. Mr. Radke seemed so surprised that Ricky showed him some of the other graphs he'd made. After studying the sheets of paper, the coach had given him a few more pointers.

"When you first start out, you'll always see a big improvement. But the better you get, the harder it gets. Instead of shaving off minutes, you shave off seconds, then tenths of seconds. Start taking every third day off. A boy your age shouldn't be running this many days in a row. You have to give your body and your mind a rest. You're still growing and developing. If you run every day, you'll mentally burn out on it; and physically you'll start getting injuries." He'd paused and smiled at Ricky. "You're doing just what you should by keeping a log. I've got to hound my boys to do it, and you're doing it all on your own and making graphs to boot. I'm going to keep my eye on you, Ricky Gordon; yes, sir, you can bet on that."

Seemed like everyone was betting on him these days, Ricky now thought as he passed the Bakers' farm pond. Matt had told him the pool on the bus was up to nine dollars and fifty cents. According to Lyle, who'd been down at the store buying Italian sandwiches with his father, ever since Diana put that BEAT THE BUS sign up in the window, even the old farts had bets going on him. "I was standing right there when Mr. Chaffee offered Mr. Mack ten bucks if he wouldn't go over the speed limit," Lyle'd said. "Everybody cracked up; I thought Duckmaker was gonna fall off the bench, he was laughing so hard. But Mr. Mack didn't think it was funny at all; he turned redder than a tomato. Said he'd been driving that bus the same way and at the same speed for twenty years without an accident, and he wasn't gonna change now."

Ricky had been relieved to hear that—beating the bus wouldn't be beating the bus if Mr. Mack drove any different.

.. ■ ..

Ricky got up with the birds on Saturday morning. He couldn't sleep; he was too excited. Today, after he was finished working at the mill and his aunt was finished with her afternoon hair appointments, he was going to Belfast to get his new running shoes. Only once had he ever owned a new pair of shoes, ones that hadn't been bought at Goodwill or retrieved from the church bin. Mrs. Lewis had given them to him for his birthday when he was seven. He still had the box they came in under his bed. He kept all his valuable things in it— his lucky marble, a Kennedy half-dollar, Mrs. Lewis' obituary: special things like that.

By the time his mother shuffled into the kitchen to make her morning coffee, he'd already done the dishes, picked up the living room, and cleaned the bathroom. "Morning, Ma."

"Another dry night," she said. "Hallelujah, hallelujah."

Ricky started laughing. He wasn't sure if it was Dr. Munsen or getting their father buried, but Matt was doing good. "Be a whole week tomorrow," he pointed out.

"Don't jinx us," she said, then knocked her knuckles on the counter.

He watched her light the stove and put the kettle on. She stood there in her ratty bathrobe, yawning, her rumpled hair looking shiny in the sunlight streaming through the kitchen window. Convincing her to let Coach Radke buy him running shoes had been tricky. His mother was funny about some things. It was okay to use food stamps, because it was "only temporary" and she "had to put food on the table," but taking charity was different. That's why she preferred Goodwill to the church bin: even if a shirt only cost a quarter, she could say she paid for it. That's why he'd picked up this morning, so she wouldn't change her mind on him and have Aunt Donna take him to Goodwill instead.

"Already been out this morning?" she asked him, dumping a spoonful of instant coffee into her mug.

"No, I wanted to wait until this afternoon. Thought I'd get up early to work on the yard some before me and Mr. Lewis went to the mill."

His mother glanced around the kitchen. "You even swept the floor. I think this running thing's been good for you, Ricky boy. I just wish I had some of your energy." She frowned and stirred her coffee. "Wish I could afford to buy you those sneakers myself."

"I told you, Ma, it ain't charity. It's like buying groceries down at the store on credit until the food stamps come in. He gives me shoes now, and when I get to high school I run for him."

"Just the same," she told him with a wistful sigh, "I wish I could."

. . ■ . .

There was the time his Aunt Donna took him to the science museum in Boston; the day Mr. Garvey had given him that geometry book, *Theorems,* and said that he could keep it; and the morning Coach Radke came all the way from Belfast just to watch him run. Right up there with those great events was getting fitted for his first pair of running shoes by a man named Barney at Downeast Sports in Belfast.

They were midnight-black with white laces and white flames along the edges of the soles. He couldn't believe how light they were, or how good they felt on his feet. If Pheidippides had been wearing a pair of these, thought Ricky, he probably wouldn't have died of exhaustion.

"He has a good fit there," Barney told Ricky's aunt. "It's a good shoe. See how easily the sole bends? If it didn't, his foot and leg muscles would have to work overtime just to flex the shoe."

"The way he runs, I just hope he doesn't wear them out too quick."

"Well, when he does, don't let his mother go out and buy him bargain shoes—they'll only buy her doctor bills. Just bring him back to me for another pair. Coach Radke wanted to make sure I told her that, let her know he'll take care of the cost. He doesn't want this kid getting stress fractures from wearing ten-dollar shoes."

"I know she talked to him the other night. But just in case he forgot to mention that, I'll tell her what you said."

While Barney and his aunt were talking, Ricky had put his old shoes back on.

"Don't you want to wear your new ones home, Ricky?" Aunt Donna asked.

"You kidding?" he said, carefully placing his new shoes back in their box. "I don't want to wreck them. These are only for running."

Chapter Ten

Usually, as soon as the afternoon bell rang, Ricky was out the door and running across the playground before any of the kids reached the school bus. But on Monday, while the kids were boarding, he did the exercises the coach had shown him to stretch and warm up his muscles. Like all Gordons, Ricky had skin that tanned easily, and while he stretched out on the school's front lawn, he noticed how dark his legs were below the rim of his shorts, and how brown his hands seemed against the white flames on his new running shoes.

"Hey, look, it's the Road Runner," sneered Bugsie. "Beep, beep."

Ricky continued with his stretches, hoping Bugsie would just leave him alone.

It was too much to hope for.

"Check out the sneakers, guys," said Bugsie as he and his gang circled around Ricky. "Where'd you steal those from, Gordon? You couldn't have found *them* in the church bin."

"Those are wicked nice," said Norman Calvert.

"Norr-mann," Bugsie said, giving his friend a warning look.

Norman shrugged. "Well, they are."

"I bet he ripped them off," said Bugsie. "Everybody knows a Gordon's middle name is Thief. Half his relatives are doing time in Thomaston and the rest are on welfare."

Ricky got up slowly, the rage that lived inside him ready to explode. A month ago, he would already have been at Bugsie's throat, but today he had a better weapon. "You think you're so great? Race me. I'll even give you a half-mile lead."

Dan Simmons, whose family lived on welfare and whose oldest brother was in the correctional center at Windham for stealing a car, said, "What about it, Bugsie?"

Bugsie had been taken off guard. He started to stammer: "I, I, can't. I have to be home in time to clean the kennels. Right, Norman?"

Before Norman had a chance to answer, the bus driver yelled, "You boys riding or what?"

Bugsie quickly took the out. "Come on, you guys! Mr. Mack's gonna leave without us!" Then he started running, but not all the crew followed as readily.

Dan Simmons lingered behind. He picked up

Ricky's backpack, and as he handed it to him, said, "Beat the bus, Ricky."

For a few seconds the two boys just stared at each other, an understanding passing between them without a word.

· · ■ · ·

When he'd tried out his new running shoes on Saturday, Ricky had felt like he was traveling at the speed of sound as he zoomed through Pine Grove Cemetery and made the loop through town. He wasn't even winded when he'd breezed by the general store and the handful of mill men who'd stopped jawing by the gas pumps just long enough to wave. He was riding a high, feeling so light-footed and confident that when he lifted his hand in return he'd almost yelled, "Better bet while you still can!" On Sunday he'd been tempted to run, but had followed Coach Radke's advice that he take every third day off in order to let his body rest and recover. And now, as he headed into his first mile, he felt strong and determined. Today would be the day.

By the time he went into his second mile, he was settled into a good pace, his arms and legs in sync, his breathing easy, his heartbeat steady, the feet inside his sneakers feeling so damned good.

During morning runs, he always put his running on automatic and allowed his mind to wander, solving problems or playing number games. But in the afternoons, he only thought about the race. *The bus is com-*

ing, the bus is coming. Elbows in, the bus is coming, hill ahead, shorter steps, lean forward. That's it, that's it. Today, however, there was something else driving him as he sped down Ridge Road under that cloudless blue sky. *Everybody knows a Gordon's middle name is Thief* . . . Those words had stirred memories of other, more painful ones. *Think you're smarter than your old man? Well, I got news for you, Momma's boy: only thing in your future's being an inmate."*

The hatred and hurt rose up inside him, tearing open that festering wound that even death couldn't heal. *If you hadn't come along, you little bastard, I wouldn't have had to marry her, wouldn't be living in a shit-hole like this. The sorriest day of my life was the day you were born.*

His stride lengthened. His arms pumped faster. His pace accelerated. He could feel the newfound fuel burning in his muscles. It rushed through his veins and rang in his ears, and he pushed all the harder. The energy inside him was so intense, he didn't think about the needling pain in his side or the stream of sweat rolling down his back. He didn't slow down for the blind curve in the road as he usually did, and didn't see the bicycle until it was suddenly right in front of him.

Tom Guimond swerved his bike toward the shoulder; Ricky swerved toward the road; both boys hit the ground at the same time.

"Where'd you come from?" yelled Tom, trying to crawl out from beneath his bike. "Jesus, Ricky, you okay?"

Dazed by the impact, Ricky wasn't sure what had hit

him. For a confused moment, he thought it was his father. *I'll give you somethin' to cry about!* He opened his eyes, saw the tar beneath his cheek, and remembered the race. He felt electricity shoot through him like a shock from a hot fence, and it jolted him right off the tar and onto his feet. Without bothering to check the damage, without even giving it a thought, he took off down the road.

"Sorry!" yelled Tom. "I hope you beat the bus!"

Ricky waved a bloodied palm in Tom's direction and kept on going. *The bus is coming, the bus is coming, the bus is coming.* He struggled to regain his rhythm but his feet were dragging, his stride was too short, his breathing was all wrong. His energy was spent.

There were still over a hundred yards to go when he heard the pummel of the tires on the road behind him. The vibrations from the bus seemed to rumble beneath his feet. With great effort, he glanced over his shoulder. It wasn't as close as he'd feared, but it was gaining fast.

Perhaps it was a surge of desperation, or that his body was conditioned to endure physical pain.

Perhaps it was his mind's stoic ability to survive mental torment—the fights and the fears and the words that cut to the bone.

Or perhaps it was just that he wanted to win so badly.

But somehow he found the strength to lift his chin off his chest and break into a full sprint.

With twenty-five yards to go, he could hear the roaring chant riding on the wind, *"Go, Ricky, go!"* The cheer pumped him up so much that when he reached his driveway he kept on going, feeling as if he could run forever.

Still, when Mr. Mack stopped the bus to let Matt off and started beeping his horn in salute, Ricky's better judgment took hold. He slowly worked himself down to a jog. Automatically, he glanced down at his watch—3:20. He'd beaten the bus fairly—numbers didn't lie.

As the bus pulled alongside of him, the new round of cheers faded. All the kids were pointing at his legs. It was only then that he noticed the trails of blood that had trickled down from the scrapes on his knees. He started to feel the road rash on his elbows and the other stings of his fall. But he continued to jog, the coach's advice coming back to him as he tried to recapture his breath. "After a run like that, son, you need to keep moving."

When the bus finally passed, Ricky glanced up at Bugsie's gang in the backseat window. A couple pointed. But only Bugsie flipped him the bird.

Sis Deans writes for children of all ages and for adults as well. She has won several regional awards, including the 1995 Maine Chapbook Award. Ms. Deans lives on a small farm in Maine with her husband and three daughters.